Caden

THE MCKEEGANS
BOOK FOUR

KATHLEEN BALL

Chapter One

Sister Laura Lee peered out from the alley. She stared one way and then the other before she pressed her back against the wooden wall. This was maddening. They could come through town any minute, or perhaps not until tomorrow. She started to peek out again, only to have a vast shadow impede her view. She stiffened, not wishing to meet who was casting the shadow.

"Can I help you with something, Sister?"

She released a shaky breath. No need to glance up. She recognized his voice. Caden McKeegan had an eerie knack for locating her. It had become outright unnerving.

She pushed her lips into what she hoped was a smile. "I don't believe I require any help right now. Thank you, Caden."

He chuckled, his voice deep. "Who are you searching for?"

"Why would you assume I was searching for anyone? I was on my way back to the orphanage when I suddenly felt fatigued. I considered maybe if I paused for a moment and, well, here we are."

He inclined his head as he examined her. "Sister, do you consider it a sin to lie?"

She granted him a smile. "Now, why are you wanting to mar a perfectly wonderful day chatting about sinning?"

The methodical clop-clop of slow-moving horses over hard ground drew her attention to the street.

The sheriff and his posse rode through town and halted in front of the sheriff's office. She tried everything except pushing Caden out of the way to have a good view. Finally, Caden stepped aside, but it was too late. They had taken the outlaw inside. She didn't recognize the horse he'd been riding, but that meant nothing.

"Did you miss something?"

She clenched her jaw. If she was the untrusting sort, she'd think Caden was following her. A frown drew on her brow. Who was she trying to fool? She *was* the untrusting sort.

"Of course not. I simply need to get back to the orphanage. So many children in need." She strode around him onto the wooden walk. He walked next to her. She walked faster, he walked faster. She slowed he slowed. Eventually, she paused, feigning to look in a window. He paused too.

"It's always nice to see you, Caden. Good day." She practically raced to the orphanage. She peered back once she got there, and Caden met her gaze. He grinned and tipped his hat to her. Of all the frustrating men!

"There you are, Sister," Mallory McKeegan declared, offering a broad smile.

"Hello, Mallory. I need to freshen up. I'll be right back." She hastened to her room, closed the door, and leaned against it. She'd planned and established a new life for herself. It had taken essentially two years of constantly changing her name and moving from town to town. She'd felt safe here in Langford, Montana. Most of the residents knew her, and none asked questions about where she had come from.

She'd taken considerable pains to establish her life and had taken care that no one learned she had once been part of the Bannock Gang or that Ed Bannock was her brother. No one here knew her last name. It had been an ominous day when Mama allowed Ed to hide his friends in the barn. *Family is family,* she'd said. Not too long after that, Mama had passed and Ed moved everyone into the small house.

Ed maintained his *little Sissy* was his good luck charm and she could never leave. None of the men had a lick of manners. Most couldn't read. All they spoke about was robbing people. They robbed stagecoaches transporting gold from the Montana mines. Later, they went after the trains.

She'd wanted no part, but once she'd overheard about the killings, she knew she had to run.

———

Caden McKeegan scrutinized the tiny nun as she ran off. Something about her had drawn him from the first. It bedeviled him he had an attraction to a nun. That was plain wrong. But he'd observed her for a bit and reached a solid conclusion: she was not a nun. He just knew it.

Since they'd met, she'd spoken one lie after another. A nun wouldn't do that, and next there was the dilemma of her name. Sister Laura Lee. That was not a nun's name. Sister

Mary, Sister Cecelia, Sister Hildegard, and Sister Catherine were names of nuns he'd known. Her eyes were too blue and her skin... Well, most nuns, he noticed, were old.

No, she wasn't a nun.

However, it didn't seem proper for him to call her on it.

He stepped toward the crowd that had assembled outside the sheriff's office. They must have someone famous inside. Even Fred Rider, the owner of the general store, had locked up and joined them.

Sheriff Stilton stood on a chair. "Listen, quiet down. The posse and I tracked down JR Bates. He's part of the Bannock outlaw gang. They pulled a job east of here. Murdered the stagecoach driver and took the gold. Any of you notice anything out of the ordinary, I need to hear about it. I don't have answers to your questions. I have telegraphs to send to find out what to do with an outlaw like this. This is a first for Langford. Leave my office and the prisoner alone!" He hopped down and moved inside.

Fred turned to Caden. "What does he mean?"

"Probably he needs to inquire about who tries the man and where. Sometimes being a territory is nice, but at other times, we don't know the specific laws."

"You're right about that, Caden." Fred clapped him on the shoulder and turned away.

Caden walked across the street, and Nolan halted his horse right before him.

"Didn't allow for any extra room when you stopped that bay," Caden remarked offhandedly. "What are you doing in town?"

"Looking for you. Where's the nun?"

4

"What nun?" Caden asked.

Nolan chuckled. "The nun you've been following the last few weeks. Where is she?"

"She's at the orphanage."

"Who'd the sheriff catch?" Nolan asked.

"An outlaw. Runs with the Bannock Gang. Last I gathered, they were in Butte." Caden shrugged.

Nolan turned his horse around. "Copper and silver are being found in Montana. Large nuggets are gushing up out of the ground."

Caden laughed. "Pull the other foot."

Chapter Two

L aura Lee opened the front door in answer to the heavy knock. Her hands tightened around her rosary. "Sheriff, how may I help you?"

"Hello, Sister. I'm hoping someone would be so kind as to deliver supper to the prisoner."

"Long line to get into the café tonight?" she asked.

"They need to make the place bigger," the sheriff complained.

"I will certainly pass your recommendation along. I'll go get the food for you now."

"Sister, I have something that needs doing. If you could just carry the food to the prisoner, I'd appreciate it. Now just give him a spoon, no forks or knives. I can't have a jailbreak."

"Where's your deputy?"

"He'll be there in an hour or so. Thank you, Sister, and tell Mallory I said thanks for the food." Sheriff Stilton tipped his hat and ambled off.

Well now... She sighed. How was she supposed to pull this off? She didn't hold hate for many, but if there was a list, JR would be at the top. He had the darkest eyes, and they were filled with pure evil. The men often brought women to the ranch, and she hadn't been allowed to interfere. But one night JR had a woman shrieking, and Laura Lee had snatched a shotgun and made him let the woman alone.

It had been the biggest mistake of her existence. JR had laughed, grabbed the shotgun from her and beat her. She could hardly get up when he finished. She had been so positive her brother would protect her, but instead, he'd lectured her and told her to stay out of their business.

For a year, she had cooked and cleaned, washed their clothes, and tended the farm while minding her business. She'd never talked to them again, and for the most part they left her be, but the fear was ever present.

Worst of all... she held no doubts that he would recognize her.

She'd have to ask someone else to take JR his food. He'd ruin her life and then some.

A meager while later, Laura Lee clutched her wrap and hastened to the café. No one else was available to take the meal to the man in jail. She smiled at Donna as she arranged the food tray. Once it was in her hands, she wanted to be sick. How was she supposed to bring this to JR? Her hands shook as she crossed the dusty street to the sheriff's office.

She was about to take the biggest risk since she had fled her brother's gang. Doing this could reveal her identity, and it had taken her so long to create the life she had. Tears filled her eyes, and she practically tripped getting onto the wooden walk. She closed her eyes and quickly prayed JR wouldn't recognize her dressed as a nun.

Swallowing hard, she willed her tears away, straightened her shoulders and entered the jail. The prisoner looked to be sleeping. What a relief. As quietly as she could, she stepped near the cell door. She put the tray on a chair near the cell and pushed it close enough for JR to reach. The chair made a loud squeak, and the next thing she knew, she was face to face with her greatest enemy.

Quickly, she glanced down at the tray. She gave it a slight push and turned away.

"Hey!"

She stiffened in fear. This was it. Her safe life was about to tumble.

"Thanks."

She strode as quickly as she could while trying to stay calm. The distance from the cell to the door felt as though it had doubled. Eventually, she reached the door, turned the knob and stepped through then closed the door behind her.

Her breathing came hard, and beads of perspiration formed on her brow. Making certain no one was watching her, she crossed the street and dashed to the orphanage. She had children to tuck in. It was tragic to see fear in their eyes. Some of the children must have been badly treated before they were brought to the orphanage. Many had been homeless before the place was built.

While being an excellent place to shelter, she'd also come to love it in Langford. Running and hiding was very wearisome. Most of the people in town weren't Catholic, which helped. There weren't many questions about being Catholic brought her way. Her parents had arranged for her to be christened as a Catholic, but that was all she knew. She read her Bible enough, but she hadn't been very active in the Catholic church.

To say her past catching up with her rattled her would be a vast understatement. After taking a few cleansing breaths, she opened the orphanage door just in time to be knocked to the floor by Jenny Wade. Another child crashed on top of them.

"Stop! What in the name of... What are you doing?"

Jenny helped the younger child to stand, and then she put her hands on her hips and stared. "Sister Laura Lee, what were you going to say? You said what in the name of but didn't finish your sentence."

Laura Lee stood, rubbing her back. "I don't know what I was going to say."

"How can you not know what you were going to say?" Jenny frowned as she continued to stare.

"Sometimes your mind goes blank. It happens," Laura Lee smiled.

"Like when I don't know the answer on a test. It happens a lot, and I get a bad mark." A frown furrowed her brow. "Adults don't get bad marks?"

"First, you can tell me why you were sliding down the banister." Laura Lee stared right back.

Fortunately, Jenny didn't choose to explain, and she glanced away. Jenny could stare for the longest time. Sometimes it was unnerving.

"Well then, let's go right back up the stairs and get ready for bed," Laura Lee directed.

Donna walked toward them. "Anyone who needs to use the outhouse line up and come with me."

Laura Lee smiled at Donna. Donna never seemed to sleep. She worked at the café, taught a few classes, and helped with bedtime. She and her husband were caretakers on the land Brayden and Mallory McKeegan had purchased. When did she find time to see her husband?

"You are a marvel, Miss Donna."

"As are you, Sister Laura Lee. Come along, children!"

Laura Lee herded the remaining children up the stairs. Each room was big enough for four beds. Thankfully, they had many unoccupied beds. It's troublesome to see the children so unhappy. Nighttime seemed to be the worst. Many had nightmares.

The older children helped the younger ones. Once they were all ready, they scurried into a big room with pillows on the floor. Each sat on a pillow and waited for story time to begin.

This was her favorite time of day, when the children had washed faces and were looking excited. She often made-up stories that would last a week. This one was about a lone bear cub and its adventures meeting other baby animals.

They hung on to her last word and all groaned when she declared it was time for bed. It was easy to forget her troubles when she was with the orphans. It was shocking how many couples came looking at the orphanage only for someone to do all the work on their farm. Didn't they realize they were children who needed love?

Jenny Wade waited by her bedroom door. "Sister, I'm sorry for the trouble I caused. Sometimes I just can't help myself."

Laura Lee drew the girl into an embrace. "All is forgiven. We all have traits we need to work on. You're just impulsive, but many young people are. Get some sleep."

Jenny pulled out of Laura Lee's arms and scooted to her bed. She was a willful child, but sometimes that was needed to get through the rough times.

Tomorrow would bring a much-needed new teacher. She'd probably get scooped up by some cowboy. One of the McKeegans, she imagined. Sighing, she went to bed.

Chapter Three

S tanding near the street, waiting for the stage to arrive, Caden tugged at his collar. Wearing Sunday clothes on a Tuesday was inexcusable. A schoolteacher was a schoolteacher, and she sure wouldn't care if his top button wasn't done up.

"Quit squirming," Mallory chastised him.

"Why couldn't Brayden be here? He lives closer, and he's your husband. To me, he's the obvious choice." Caden yanked at his collar again.

Mallory slapped his hand. "You know very well Brayden and Myles are meeting with a buyer today. It was your pa's idea for you to be here to welcome the teacher. I'll be certain to request Nolan next time."

Caden released a loud guffaw. "You think Nolan would want to wear his Sunday clothes in the middle of the week? He'd have ridden in the other direction at the first mention."

Thundering hooves raised a cloud of dust at the end of the street.

"Here's the stage now." As the stagecoach drew near, Mallory grabbed Caden's arm, her face showing alarm. "Oh, no! Something's wrong! The driver looks like he's hurt. I'll run and fetch the doctor and let Sheriff Stilton know." She hurried off before he could protest.

The coach slowed, and the driver slumped, ready to fall over. Caden swiftly hauled himself onto the seat. Blood oozed from a hole in the driver's arm. The sticky redness was everywhere, saturating the man's shirt, dripping off the seat. Quickly, Caden grabbed his bandana out of his pocket and tied it around the wound on the driver's arm as tight as he could.

A crowd of people had gathered, and Caden handed the driver down to two men who then hurriedly carried him toward the doc.

Caden climbed down and heard a whimper. Hadn't anyone bothered to look inside? He yanked the door open and found a woman huddled on the floor. Another male passenger was slumped across the seat, clearly dead.

"You must be the new schoolteacher." He held out his hand. She took so long to take it; he was relatively positive she wouldn't.

At last she slipped her hand into his, and gently, he helped her out of the coach. She wobbled a bit, and he put his hands on her shoulders.

"Were you hit?" Caden asked.

She just stared at him.

"Did you get shot?" he asked.

"No, I got down when the driver yelled for us to. Oh, my. What? Oh..." Her eyes closed and Caden caught her, instantly scooping her up.

"This way, Caden!" Sister Laura Lee yelled.

Caden searched the crowd, spotted her, and nodded. He carried the teacher to the orphanage and followed the sister to an unoccupied room. He placed her on the bed.

"She claimed they did not shoot her."

"That's good to hear." Sister Laura Lee poured water into the basin next to the bed. She plucked a cloth down from a shelf and wet it. Sitting on the bed, she washed the woman's face.

"I'm assuming she's the new teacher. She's older than I imagined," Sister Laura Lee commented.

"She seems young enough to me," Caden replied.

"I thought she was fresh from earning her teacher's certificate. I didn't mean she was old, old."

Caden laughed. "As old as Moses?"

"I don't get it," the sister replied.

"It's just that all the nuns I've ever seen were as old as Moses. It was funny at the time."

She grinned. "I'm sure it was at the time."

Embarrassment swept over him. Anything he said about it now would just add to it. It had been funny at the time. He went to the window to gather his wits about him. He wanted to laugh but couldn't. After getting himself together, he turned toward the bed.

Sister Laura Lee resembled a beautiful angel. His breath caught. Looking at nuns with the things he was thinking wasn't allowed. Even if he wasn't convinced she was really a nun. He averted his gaze and stared at the teacher instead. She wasn't hard on the eyes. Her bonnet was still on, and her eyes were closed. She was attractive enough, he supposed. Then again, he shouldn't be thinking about the teacher that way, either.

"Do you think she'll wake up shortly?" he inquired.

"She was awake when you first carried her out of the stagecoach. That's a positive sign. I'm confident someone will send Doc over when he's finished with the driver."

"Must have been a robbery. I wonder if it has anything to do with that fella in jail."

"I wouldn't know." Her voice sounded irritated.

"I'm sorry. Nolan claims I babble. I hope the doc comes soon. Do you know her name or where she's from?"

"Mariah Culkin, and she's from a small town in Ohio. That's all I know."

"Mariah, Miss Culkin, can you hear me?" Caden asked. He nodded when he noted a faint frown form on her brow. "She's stirring a bit."

"That's always a favorable sign," Sister Laura Lee said. This time, her voice was calm.

The woman opened her eyes and looked terrified. "Oh, my... Where am I? What happened?"

"You fainted when they brought you off the stagecoach. Do you recall anything?" Sister Laura Lee asked.

The woman's expression was troubled. "There were two men who rode up and shot the driver. Oh! One passenger was shot too. It was so unbelievably awful." She bit her lip then drew a deep breath. "He's dead, isn't he?"

"Yes, ma'am," Caden told her. "The driver is with the doc right now. Doc'll be by to check on you promptly."

"I'm Sister Laura Lee, and this gentleman is Caden McKeegan. Right now, you are at the orphanage. So, you're in the correct place but not the right room. The children created pictures for you and tacked them on the wall. It's a lovely room. You can see it once the doc finishes checking you over."

"It's nice to meet you both. No one mentioned the school is run by nuns," Mariah said.

"It's not. I'm just a stray. We have a lovey pastor, and we have a Christian church. Often, out west, there is only one church in each town. We make do. It is The Lord's House after all."

"I didn't mean to offend you. My hometown had a Christian church too. All were welcome." She sat up. "I'm feeling better. They shoved my bags to the ground. The robbers took a big metal box, though. They were glad they brought the wagon with them. The man traveling with me had a trial getting his gun out of the holster and his hand shook when he fired it. He fell backward. Next, he got up and stuck his head out the window. It shocked me he didn't get shot then. But suddenly he put his head and gun out the window and he was shot. I don't know who he was."

"He didn't give you a name?" Caden asked.

"No, I introduced myself, but he ignored me. City slicker, most likely." She smiled at them. Clearly, she wasn't one for hysterics.

17

"Here you are!" Mallory declared cheerfully upon entering the room. "I'm Mallory and you must be Mariah. I see you met Sister Laura Lee and my brother-in-law Caden."

"Yes, they have been very kind," Mariah told her.

"I'll sit with you while we wait for the doctor," Mallory announced.

"I have plenty of children to tend," Sister Laura Lee added.

"Nice to meet you, ma'am," Caden said. He followed the sister out the door.

Chapter Four

Her brother was getting closer. She could sense it in her bones.

"Sister, wait!" Caden called to her.

She turned and waited for him to catch up to her.

"Thank you for all your help. Are you all right? If you're frightened because of the recent violence, I can assure you Sheriff Stilton has a posse out searching for those outlaws. Keep the children away from the front of the building just to be safe." He came to a stop in a shuffling of feet. "And... if there is anything I can do for you..."

"It's nice to have a new teacher. You realize she is not married. She's a pretty woman, don't you think?" She craned her neck, glancing up at him.

Caden shrugged his right shoulder. "I suppose so. My mind was on other things."

"Like what?"

Caden frowned. "First, I wanted to be certain she hadn't been seriously hurt. Next, I wondered who did it. Then I speculated about where they could hole up; and then I hoped they don't come to town. Why all the questions about Mariah?"

Her face warmed. "Just making conversation. It was a blessing you were here to help. Be careful out there." She wore what she hoped was an innocent sort of disinterested expression.

"Well, I'll see you later." He turned and walked off.

Laura Lee hurried to her room and snatched up her Bible. As she walked to church, she carried it close to her heart. She needed to confess her sins, and Pastor Melon would have to do.

She strolled down the walk, staring at the wooden boards beneath her feet, hoping no one would speak to her. Luckily, she made it. Pastor Melon had just entered the church. Her timing couldn't have been better.

"Sister, how are you?"

She automatically put her hand out to dip her finger in holy water to bless herself, forgetting there wasn't a font in this church. The pastor smiled at her. She crossed herself and then went to the altar, kneeled, and crossed herself again. Finally, she stood and walked to the pew where the pastor stood waiting for her.

"I'm fine, Pastor Melon. How are you?"

"I'm quite well," he responded. He swept his hand toward the pew. "Please, have a seat and you can tell me what's on your mind."

She hesitated. Perhaps she should leave. He wasn't a priest. She sat down. "Pastor, you won't tell anyone what I tell you?"

A gentle smile graced his face. "Your secrets are safe with me."

Laura Lee nodded. "It's a long story. I hope you have time."

"Of course, I do."

"I'm not a nun." There, she'd said it.

The pastor didn't seem surprised. He merely nodded.

"You knew?"

"Not at first. You know your Bible, and you dress like a nun, but you never have the serenity of most of the nuns I've met.: He angled his head and fixed her in his gaze. "You're troubled. I really didn't know for certain, but the thought that you are not who you say you are has crossed my mind."

"I have my reasons, but, Pastor, what would God think?" She squeezed the rosary in between her hands. "My name is Laura Lee Bannock. My brother is the leader of the Bannock Gang."

"Are you aiming to break that outlaw out of jail?"

She shook her head. "I've been hiding from my brother for two years now. I kept changing my name and appearance. His gang moved into our home when our mother died. He forced me to cook and clean for them. I didn't have anywhere else to go. I was afraid. JR, the man in jail, wound up striking me, so I ran away. The last place I was at, there was a kind nun. We exhausted nearly every way for me to hide for good. I realized if I wed, they would shoot my husband down."

Taking a deep breath, she continued. "Sister Teresa knew I was christened Catholic, and we went over what that meant before she offered me her clothes. I wasn't confident it was the right thing to do. We prayed on it for many days, and then the sister told me to go with God's blessing. It was a blessing. It got me out of town, and no one followed me or found me. But, Pastor, what about the lies I tell to continue the ruse?"

"That is a conundrum. I expect that Sister Teresa was right about having God's blessing. A blessing of protection, if you will. Of course, lying is a sin, but in this instance, I assume it's still for your protection. I haven't seen you practicing any church observances. But I can pray for you." He studied her for a moment. "You can't ask God's absolution, I'm afraid, for something you intend to continue doing. My suggestion would be to thank the Lord for His blessings and protection. I would also make God aware that you recognize you are lying, and you realize it is wrong. He might help so you no longer have to lie."

"Thank you."

"The blessing from the nun is key," he reminded her. "You aren't seeking to harm anyone. You aren't seeking to convert anyone to become Catholic. In this town, you have done an abundance of good. Remember, there will be those who will feel betrayed. Stay safe, Sister."

"You called me sister."

His lips lifted in a smile. "I'm with Sister Teresa on this. It's for your protection from evil."

Chapter Five

"You should see your face," Nolan stated. "It looks like you've been thinking too hard."

Caden grinned. "That's because I am thinking hard. In fact, it's extremely complicated thinking."

"Thinking too hard can lead to brain damage. You know, like being dropped on your head." Nolan shook his head.

"Just because it happened to you doesn't mean the same for me," Caden teased.

"Seriously, Caden, what's going on?"

Caden got off his horse and waited for Nolan to do the same. They both dropped the reins and peered out over the north valley where their crossbred cattle grazed. They'd spent a long while in Texas learning about cattle breeding.

"It's a beautiful sight, brother. I'm glad we made the trip to Texas," Caden observed. They were fine bulky cattle and should bring a high price when auctioned.

"Changing the subject? Is the new teacher pretty? I heard she's a bit long in the tooth."

"If you consider around twenty to be long in tooth, then yes. Actually, I thought we'd be getting a young girl right out of school. She's attractive. Sister Laura Lee seemed to like her."

"Aha! It always comes back to the nun. You realize you can't court a nun, don't you?"

"I'd heard that mentioned a time or two." Caden took off his hat and wiped his brow. "The nun is always around, it seems. I still can't get over her name... Laura Lee."

"I understand you must have the whole changing their name wrong. I wonder if she has hair."

Caden laughed. "Of course, she has hair under that... that thing she wears. You know, her nun clothes."

"Ma would have had a fit listening to us. She was raised with nuns. Remember how we hid the first time a nun visited? We thought they all carried a switch." Nolan chuckled.

"I sure miss Ma. Maybe I'll find me a nice girl to settle down with some day."

"Listen to you!" Nolan subjected him to a suspicious sideways glance. "You're not staking a claim on the teacher, are you? I haven't had a chance to meet her."

"Quit your fretting. You're like an old hen. Nope, I don't know her enough to stake any claim. I'm not certain if she'll be at the orphanage fund raising dance or not," Caden said with a shrug.

"I bet your nun will be there," Nolan added.

Caden quickly pulled his hat over his head, mounted his horse, and left without another word. Sometimes Nolan was fun, but at other times he was a genuine pain.

The orphanage had originally started out as a hotel that had never been completed. Brayden and Mallory had the whole place remodeled, which included a vast space where tables could be pushed to the side, and they could hold a dance.

"Pastor Melon, are you sure I need to be here? I mean, I can't dance. I'd rather be upstairs telling the children stories."

"Sister, these fund raisers are for the orphans and the church. People would expect you to be here. How is your praying coming along?"

Laura Lee smiled. "The Lord and I speak hourly. There are so many blessings here. Being with the children provides a lifetime of blessings. I have apologized for the lying, but I didn't ask to be forgiven yet. It's amazing how a sense of peace comes over me after I pray."

"It is miraculous. Do you need help with the punch?"

"I think it's all set. I don't understand why there is one bowl near the cookies and another on a different table. It's puzzling." She shook her head.

"One is for the children, and one is for the older members of the church to guard. Occasionally the punch gets spiked." He grinned.

"Spiked?" she inquired.

"Adding alcohol."

"Spirits can be the very devil," she declared, shaking her head. The men she'd known had become violent when they partook. "I shall guard it, Paster."

"I was wondering if you two would show up," Myles said.

"Dances aren't my favorite," Caden commented.

"We're here to watch the pretty girls," Nolan confessed.

Their oldest brother, Aiden, stood behind them, chuckling. "Some things never change," he remarked with a grin.

"So, where is the new teacher?" Nolan asked, scanning the crowd.

"Her name is Mariah, and she is guarding the punch with the sister," Aiden told them.

Caden furrowed his brow. "Guarding?"

Myles grinned. "So no one will spike it."

Caden laughed. "Most men have flasks. I bet Old Tucker Jones has moonshine to sell outside somewhere."

"I'm going to meet her," Nolan left.

Caden followed and managed to get around his brother, reaching the two women first.

"Sister, you look well. Miss Culkin, you look much better than the last time we met." Caden gave them a pleasant smile. He could almost see the steam coming out of Nolan's ears.

"Good evening, Sister Laura Lee. Miss Culkin, it's a pleasure to meet you. I'm Nolan McKeegan." Nolan had never been so polite.

"It's nice to meet you, Nolan and Caden. It's good to see you again. Please call me Mariah."

"Thank you, Mariah." Nolan took her hand and held it for a moment.

Caden wanted to, but he controlled himself.

"Any attempt to spike the punch?" Caden asked Sister Laura Lee.

She laughed. "You don't expect anyone will try with a nun standing next to it, do you? In fact, I believe the consumption of punch is considerably less than normal."

Caden nodded. "It is quiet over here. You do know they buy moonshine right outside, don't you?"

"Mr. McKeegan, I'm not that naïve. I'm here to protect the punch, not the men's souls."

"Mariah, may I have this dance?" Nolan requested.

"Of course," she replied.

Caden and the sister watched the other two leave.

"Your brother is very well mannered."

"Compared to who?" Caden scowled.

"I haven't seen him scowl yet," she smiled.

"He must think Mariah is pretty," he commented

"And you don't."

"There's nothing wrong with the way she looks. I guess she's pleasant enough to look at."

She turned and stared at him. "You don't want a wife?"

"I did, but lately I've come to the conclusion I want a woman I can be friends with, someone who I can love and loves me back. I want a wife who is trustworthy. It might be too much to ask, but I'm willing to wait."

Chapter Six

Every time she saw Caden, he surprised her. had he really said, *"I want a woman I can be friends with, someone who I can love and loves me back. I want a wife who is trustworthy. It might be too much to ask, but I'm willing to wait."*

Apparently, Caden was a romantic, and she never would have guessed. The dance last night had continued on for overly long. Every time someone entered, she became apprehensive. Her brother Ed was bound to show up. Sooner or later she would see him again. Would he kill her when he found her? He sure had vowed he would.

Acting like a nun had protected her thus far, but did she blend in? She wanted to be in the background as someone no one paid attention to. Then again, her brother might expect lightning to strike him if he got too close to a nun.

One thing was for sure, she needed to collect items she would require for living on the run for a while. Would Mr. Rider consider it strange if she bought a bedroll and a canteen? Yes, he likely would. She must take them from a cowboy. Her sins were piling up, and her heart grew heavy.

She'd check horses this evening. Someone might have what she needed. Walking out of her room, she could hear Mariah's voice. She was teaching. She had a kind way about her. The children seemed to like her, and that was what mattered.

Leaving was going to be heartbreaking. That was possibly her punishment for her lies.

Screaming and yelling outside caught her attention. She ran to the door and opened it. The horses from the approaching stagecoach sounded winded and sweaty. When it stopped, a woman practically fell out the door.

Floyd Rider caught her before she hit the ground. Next, a well-dressed man exited the stage. He looked as though he belonged in a city like New York instead of the Wild West. He held a small book in his hand in which he quickly began writing. Was he a reporter? The man glanced her way and narrowed his eyes.

Mallory escorted the woman into the café. What a relief! She had a strange feeling she shouldn't go outside.

Then she saw him. Her brother's hands were tied in front of him as he sat on a horse. Sheriff Stilton and many men she recognized from town surrounded him. Closing her eyes, she swallowed hard. When she opened her eyes, Ed Bannock stared at her. He knew, oh no, he knew. As fast as lightning she closed the door and leaned against it. Now what?

She didn't have a horse to ride or gear to take with her when she left. But she couldn't stay in town. Ed might be behind bars, but he'd still find a way to get to her... to kill her. A chill swept up her spine. She couldn't stick around.

She took a pillowcase and put in her few items. Next, she took a few apples and an empty glass jar. After slipping out the back door, she filled the jar with water and placed it all in her pillowcase bag. Slipping into the woods behind the buildings was easy enough. Everyone was in front where all the excitement was.

From a safe distance, she turned and gazed at the town. It was the nicest home she'd had in a long while. She'd even made friends. Glancing at the sun, she continued north. There might be fewer people in the north since the winters were supposedly much worse.

Keeping in the woods, she walked for hours until it was dusk. There was a farmhouse up ahead and clothes on the clothesline, swinging back and forth in the hearty breeze. Did she dare? Did she have a choice? Ed would most likely get the word out that she was dressed as a nun.

Edging ever so slowly toward the clothesline, she examined the clothes. Boys' pants and a shirt looked like it would be the best fit. She quickly swiped them off the line and headed back into the woods. After gently folding her clothes, she put on the pants and shirt. It was beyond scandalous.

She'd either need a hat or something to cut her hair. If she'd planned ahead, she would have a knife. Tucking her hair into the back of her shirt seemed to be the best option for now.

She walked until it was too dark to see. She'd been looking for a place to sleep, and the best she found was an enormous willow tree. It took a lot of effort to climb the tree, but it was well worth it. Later, three pairs of eyes watched her.

The wolves stayed most of the night, but she remained relatively safe and out of their reach.

"A Pinkerton? We haven't had one of those come to town in years," Caden said.

Breakfast was more boisterous than usual with everyone trying to get more information.

"It's serious business; people are getting hurt," his pa commented. "If you were home for supper, you would have met him. His name is John Sanders. He said he has a lead on a family member of Ed Bannock's gang in town. Supposedly been living here for a while. I couldn't think of anyone."

"I was pulling a cow out of a mud pit. It took me longer than I'd thought. Too bad I missed him." Caden rubbed his hand over his face. "The last Pinkerton was a small guy who arrested the wrong man. I hope this one is better."

Aiden nodded. "He seemed to know his stuff. A bit mysterious, though. He wouldn't give any hints about the family member."

"Really? Young or old? What about male or female? Those are things people need to know if he wants help." Caden shook his head.

"Nolan went to town early to see what he could find out. I doubt he'll discover anything," his pa told them.

"I don't know." Caden shrugged. "Nolan is nosier than an old maid."

Christy laughed. "Mama, are old maids nosey?"

Erieann gave him a sharp glance. "Not nosier than most folks."

Caden stood up. He was going to laugh any minute, and that would presumably cause Erieann to be mad.

"I'll be in the foothills gathering strays. Let Nolan know work comes first." He left with a smile on his face. Nolan was a hard worker, and he wouldn't appreciate the comment.

Chapter Seven

Laura Lee groaned. It took a long while to work out the kinks in her body. She'd tied herself to the tree and had been able to obtain a bit of sleep here and there. It had been a terrifying night. Every time she woke the wolves were circling the tree. They would jump and scratch the trunk. Thankfully, she was high enough they never reached her and her knots held.

This wouldn't do. No one would think of her as a boy. What a pickle to be in. For now, she had no choice but to continue walking. After checking the position of the sun, she began her trek. She ate very little of her precious food and drank only a mouthful of her water. If only she were familiar with the area. Not knowing if there was a way to get water could be her downfall.

She hiked for hours and didn't see another soul. Her safety wore heavily on her. There was no way for her to defend herself. Oh, why, hadn't she brought a knife?

Something ahead drew her eye. Were those berries? She walked faster into the bushes and was hopeful for the first time that day. They were a beautiful sight. The juice of the berries rolled down her chin until finally she stopped. Would the berries be fine if she filled the pillowcase, or would they just get smooshed? Gently, she placed them on top. The stains wouldn't show on her nun's clothing.

But now she'd become a target for all flies in Montana. Shooing them away didn't help. Finally, she wet a corner of the pillowcase with water and cleaned her chin. She had no business being out in the woods alone. Her choices had come to possibly being eaten by an animal or being shot by her brother and his gang.

Lord, I've placed myself in an impossible situation. Please allow me to locate a town. No matter what I do, it'll be a lie. I'm not a boy or a nun. I am a child of God, and the thought of that makes me brave.

She trudged all day, and just before dusk, she spotted a farm. Maybe she could sneak into the barn to sleep? And oh, blessed mercy! There was a well. Cool water would be a delight. A big rock sat just inside the tree line. From there, she could watch the front of the house.

The place looked well maintained. There were flowers in front of the porch. Two rocking chairs looked out on a small flower garden. It was peaceful. There was probably a vegetable garden nearby. Her heart panged. Her sins would soon be too many to surmount.

A lamp was lit inside the house. She could see two people, a man and woman. The man looked small. Perhaps he was just a boy. Were they waiting for the father to arrive? Her stomach growled as they put a pot in the middle of the table and then sat. They said grace and then helped themselves to the food.

They didn't seem to be waiting for anyone. There wasn't another plate on the table. Dare she knock on the front door? Perhaps if she told them the truth... It would be doubtful that would happen. She reached into her case for the jar of water.

"Hands up, you varmint."

Laura Lee jumped at the deep voice behind her.

"Planning to steal something?" The stranger snorted. "Not much to steal."

Slowly, she turned with her hands over her head. "No, yes, I was hoping to sleep in your barn tonight. I can't stand the thought of wolves trying to get at me all night."

The dark-haired man lowered his rifle. "You're female? Hard to tell with your hair stuffed down the back of your shirt. You running away from home?"

"Something like that." Before she knew it, she spilled the entire story.

"The Bannock Gang? Let's get you inside and fed. Then we can try to figure out a plan for you."

Relief ran through her as she followed the man to the house. He opened the door and ushered her in.

He turned toward her. "I didn't even ask your name."

"Laura Lee," she replied. She smiled, and the woman narrowed her eyes.

"Laura Lee, I'm Gideon Strong. This is my mother Sharon and..." His eyes lit up when he looked at the boy. "This is my son Felix."

"It's nice to meet you," she said politely.

"Why is she here?" Sharon demanded.

"She ran into a bit of trouble and needs a place for now."

"Where is she supposed to sleep?" Sharon's voice grew louder.

A chill ran down Laura Lee's back. She should leave. "I can sleep in the barn, and I'll be gone in the morning."

"Let's all sit and have supper. Mother, could you set two more places please?"

Sharon set two more places, grumbling the whole time.

"I don't wish to cause trouble. I'll just go." The smell of roasted meat tempted her, but she wasn't wanted.

"Everyone sit, bow your heads, and we'll pray," Gideon insisted.

She hardly heard his prayer. Her throat grew tight, feeling Sharon's ardent gaze upon her. "So, Laura Lee, do the women wear trousers where you come from?"

"No, ma'am. The only other clothing I have is my nun outfit. And I couldn't very well go traipsing through the woods wearing it." Oh no, Sharon had her so rattled she didn't know what she was saying.

Sharon relaxed and beamed. "Imagine that, a nun. God is surely mysterious."

It was Felix's turn to frown. "I thought nuns cut off all their hair."

"Some do. If I was residing at a convent, I would certainly have short hair."

"You can change after supper," Sharon informed her.

Her face heated.

"You look like a tomato," Felix declared.

"Felix—"

She put her hand up. "It's fine. I probably do look very much like a tomato." She glanced at Sharon. "I'm afraid my clothes need proper washing and airing."

"We can plan to do that tomorrow." Sharon smiled.

Laura Lee dared to glance at Gideon. He must think her the worst of liars. The look he gave her reassured her. She'd figure out a way to talk to him tonight.

"You have a lovely home. I always wished for pretty curtains."

"That would be Millie's doing. She died a few years back. Do you think God would disapprove?"

Food got stuck in her throat for a minute. "Disapprove about what?" Laura Lee inquired.

"You know the showy pattern, or the bright colors Millie used to decorate?"

"Were you too prideful showing the curtains to everyone? Other than that, there isn't a thing wrong with making a place cheery." What if Sharon continued asking about what God would think? She'd surely have to leave.

"Laura Lee probably doesn't choose to air her faults, but she's no longer a nun. I have a feeling she is too embarrassed to tell you," Gideon remarked.

Sharon put her hand to her chest. "What?"

Laura Lee grabbed her glass and drank her water while trying to come up with an answer. She set the glass down and gazed right at Sharon.

"I had too many moments of doubt. So many things happened to me, which I'd rather not talk about. I turned from the Lord. I wasn't sure I could serve Him in the way He deserved." She stared down at her plate. "I've regained my faith, but one can't be a nun then quit and expect to become a nun again."

"Then why carry the clothes of a nun?" Sharon asked.

"For safety. It's wrong, I know that. My brother is on the wrong side of the law. He always told me if I left home, he'd kill me. Of course, I had to get away. He followed, but I managed to get away. I joined the convent, and I didn't see him again. Now he's robbing trains and asking around about me." She breathed in deeply. "The last place I lived at was an orphanage where I taught and tended the children. I entered the town as a nun, and it seemed safer. I know you must think I'm horrible, but I didn't know what else to do. One of his gang got arrested, and I knew my brother would be coming. So I left, and here I am." Her eyes filled with tears. At least there was more truth than lies in what she said.

She was so tired of being frightened and alone, always looking over her shoulder.

"My dear, you poor woman. You'll be safe here for at least a little while."

"Thank you. I'm not deserving of your understanding. You are very kind."

"You don't have to worry. Pa and I will protect you!" Felix declared.

She smiled kindly at the youth. He looked much like his father, with his dark hair and eyes. He was perhaps twelve? She was no good at judging a person's age.

"Gideon, after we're done in the kitchen, will you bring some water to heat it on the stove? Laura Lee, you can have a nice bath, and I'll find you a night rail. I bet some of my dresses I've outgrown would fit you. Nothing fancy, mind you."

A smiling Sharon was much better than the suspicious Sharon.

Chapter Eight

L aura Lee had grown used to being interrupted when she
slept. The children at the orphanage knew they could
come to her. Nothing, not even a screaming newborn, was
louder than Sharon.

Sharon offered to share her bed and it was a nice offer. But the
household must hear her each night. Sharon snored and then
snorted extra loud and sat up.

Laura Lee closed her eyes, pretending to sleep. It would have
been nice if Sharon rose for the day and Laura Lee could sleep
another hour. That didn't happen.

"Rise and shine! This is a day the Lord has made. Let us give
Him thanks and praise!" Sharon certainly was chipper in the
morning.

"Yes, let us count our blessings and give Him praise indeed."
Laura Lee sat up.

Sharon put on a bathrobe, and deposited clothes at the end of the bed. "I thought I'd let you get dressed first while I put on coffee. I'll get changed when you're done."

"That's very kind of you, thank you." As soon as Sharon left, Laura Lee shot out of bed. She immediately picked up the blue gingham dress. It was clean and well mended. She put it on and laughed. Two of her could have fit in the dress. Somehow, though, she'd make it work. In fact, the dress was nicer than any she'd worn before.

What would it be like to live a nice fear-free life? No more lying, she promised. She'd pray for forgiveness if it actually happened. She'd pray on it.

She felt self-conscious when she stepped out of the bedroom. Her hands tightly clasping the extra fabric on each side of her.

"Don't you look lovely. Now, I know the dress is a bit big but much better than those trousers," Sharon said. "Don't you think?"

"Yes, ma'am, thank you. I can finish making breakfast, so you can get dressed," Laura Lee offered.

Sharon glanced at Gideon and smiled. "That would be a blessing. Thank you."

What was that smile all about? Laura Lee quickly made herself at home in the kitchen. She scrambled eggs and took the biscuits out of the oven. Freshly made butter was on the counter.

"How about a refill?" she asked as she brought the coffee pot to the table.

"I'd love some," Felix said.

"Good try. I would like some though." Gideon watched her the whole time, and she couldn't decide if she was uncomfortable due to her shyness or because he was a man.

"Thank you."

"Should I wait for your mother before setting out the food?"

"Wait. We don't want a grumpy grandma," Felix teased.

"I heard that, Felix." Sharon stepped into the kitchen. "I'll have you know I have never had a grumpy moment."

Gideon and Felix exchanged glances but didn't say a word.

Sharon helped set out the food, and when everyone was seated, they said grace.

"Look Grandma, nothing is burned. Not like when—"

"We don't need to talk about that woman. Laura Lee, do you do much cooking?"

"Yes, when I can. I always cooked growing up and before I left home. The orphanage had its share of cooks, so I mainly taught, read bedtime stories, and comforted the little ones. It was nice to cook again."

Sharon gave her a hearty nod. "When you lived at home, did you do all the housework?"

"Ma, let her be. She doesn't need to list the duties she's capable of doing."

"I will absolutely work hard while I'm here. I can leave anytime you want. I did the housework, all of it. I put in a big garden and tended the horses and the few head of cattle we had. I can hunt too, if you like." She smiled. Whoever burned meals mustn't have pulled her weight.

"What about sewing?"

"Yes, ma'am, I'm good with a needle."

Sharon lightly slapped the table. "You can take the dresses in. I have plenty more. Oh, this is delightful having another woman in the house."

Laura Lee glanced at Gideon. The was a combination of anger and hurt in his eyes. She was going to have to step lightly. She'd only stay until tomorrow and let this family get back to normal.

———

Caden walked into the house and set his hat on the table. "He's a Pinkerton for sure. For some reason he's after Sister Laura Lee. Come to find out the sister hasn't been seen in days. What kind of trouble could she be in that a Pinkerton is looking for her?"

His father nodded. "Pastor Mellon is stopping by. He told me he had a lot to say. He didn't want to betray her trust. But he thinks she's in danger."

"Danger? When's he coming? Maybe I should ride to his house."

"Now settle down, Caden," admonished his pa. "He said he'd be here early afternoon so it could be anytime now. Plus, he didn't specifically say he wanted everyone to know."

Caden nodded. "I wouldn't tell anyone outside of the family."

"If he doesn't want to include you, don't show any anger. He doesn't have to say a thing, but he's concerned."

"You look tired, Pa."

Eion chuckled. "I played outside with Christy all morning. She has so much energy and her imagination is wild. We had fun but I'm not a young man anymore."

Their foreman Pierce opened the door and stepped inside, followed by Pastor Mellon. Pierce nodded toward Eion.

"Pastor, good to have you here. I know Nessa and Mary Jane are busy getting coffee and refreshments. Why don't you take a seat."

"Good to see you Eion, you too, Caden. We might as well get started before I change my mind. I've gone back and forth on what's the right thing. Her safety comes first. I'm glad you're here, Caden. I know she'd especially fond of you."

There wasn't much said until after the two women had brought the coffee and shortbread cakes then left.

"This will be a shock to you," began Pastor Mellon, "but Laura Lee is not a nun."

"What do you mean? Of course, she is," Caden said. But in his mind, he thought about all of the doubts he'd had.

The pastor held up his hand. "Wait and listen. Her last name is Bannock, and Ed Bannock is her brother. She kept house for him, and then his gang moved in. She wanted to leave but Ed threatened to kill her if she ever left. The men weren't exactly gentleman, and she was frightened.

"One day she escaped but wherever she went her brother was not far behind. She went from town to town, and one day a nun took her in. They became close, and the nun advised Laura Lee to pretend to be a nun. I know it sounds crazy but the nun prayed on it and felt it was the right thing to do. Laura Lee knows her Bible, and apparently she *is* Catholic. She worried about the lies, though. I advised her to do what would keep her safe. I believe she ran when the first of the Bannock Gang was arrested." He took a sip of coffee. "I don't trust the Pinkerton. He didn't seem to have Laura Lee's best interest at heart."

Caden sat back, stunned. It was though someone had hit him over his head. Not a nun? She lied to him. The whole time he'd known her she had lied. Even though he had suspected something was not right about her story, hearing the truth hit him like a bullet between the eyes. His heart wrenched. No. He needed to stop. This wasn't about him.

"What can we do to keep her safe?" Caden asked after a few moments.

Eion stood. "We need to find her before anyone else does."

"Pastor, do you have any inclination where she might have gone?" Caden asked. His mind raced with possibilities.

"She wasn't seen leaving town. She could be anywhere, but she probably headed into the woods until she was certain she was far enough away. I checked and she didn't take the coach. The Pinkerton fella has questioned most of the town. Most folks think he's crazy. They can't believe Laura Lee isn't a nun. I've had a few people ask me what I thought. I just say she seemed very nun-like to me. I just hope she's disguised herself as someone else. I'm glad you're here Caden. I know you two have some sort of bond."

Surprised, Caden stared at Pastor Mellon, mouth gaping.

"You two are drawn to one another. I saw it every time you were in the same vicinity. Thinking her a nun, you probably pushed it out of your mind." His eyes twinkled. "I need to get back to town. I have to find a way to have the Pinkerton search in the wrong direction."

"Thanks for stopping by," Eion said as he stood and then walked the pastor to the door.

Caden's mind whirled. Where could she be? Did she know anyone in a nearby town? He didn't know Laura Lee at all. He didn't even know what color hair she had. The pastor had been right when he said they were drawn to one another, but guilt had always filled him. He'd thought her married to God.

"What's the plan?" his father asked.

"I don't have one."

Shaking his head, Eion sighed. "Caden I'd have to say that's a first."

Chapter Nine

It had been a while since Laura Lee had done manual labor. Her muscles hurt, but her heart was full of accomplishment. The laundry was drying on the line, and the garden had been weeded. Next, she'd help with supper. It was the type of life she'd lived before Ed invited his gang to live at their home. After they'd moved in, her workload had grown and grown until all she felt was resentment.

Here, she was thanked and was on the other end of many smiles. She hadn't looked over her shoulder once. Gideon made her feel safe. He was a nice man. He'd been married twice before. His first wife died giving birth to Felix. His second wife, Millie up and left. Sharon hadn't liked her. Gideon never mentioned her, but Sharon had given her an earful.

According to Sharon, Millie had been trouble from the first. She didn't do much to help around the farm. She spent too much time in town and never took to Felix. Gideon had felt sorry for the woman or something.

It was no secret Sharon wanted Laura Lee for Gideon. In another time, she'd have jumped at the chance, but there was a possibility she'd have to up and run. She didn't love Gideon, but they would have gotten on well together. Truthfully, there was another man she missed. Try as she might, she couldn't get him out of her mind. It wasn't as though she'd see him again.

"You look pensive," Gideon commented.

"I suppose I do. I keep thinking I might bring trouble to you."

"No one knows you're here. You stayed home when we attended church, so I doubt anyone has a clue. Tomorrow I'll go to the general store, sit with some of the older men and read a few newspapers. The Bannock Gang is well known. There might be information."

"Gideon, I'm sure you noticed how your mother…"

"Keeps throwing us together?" He chuckled. "Don't mind her. She wants more grandchildren. I'm not ready to be married again. For all I know I'm still married to Millie. I would like your friendship, though."

"You already have that." She smiled up at him.

He stiffened. "Go inside and hide like we practiced. Now."

She walked quickly to the house. Once inside she whispered to Sharon, who followed her into Gideon's bedroom. They opened the trunk at the end of his bed, and she folded herself down into it. Once there Sharon put bedding and a few other items on top of her.

"Be silent and safe," Sharon whispered.

"Mother, would you be so kind to pour Mr. Sanders here a cup of coffee. He's come a long way searching for some female." Gideon's voice was louder than usual.

"Who else lives here?"

"My mother, my son, and I."

"There are two sizes of dresses out on the line."

Laura Lee's stomach churned. She put her hand over her mouth to stay quiet.

"Those belong to Gideon's errant wife. She's been gone long enough I decided to sell her clothes. I'll get a better price if they are clean and ironed. One needs mending."

"Where is your son?"

"Now, wait a minute. I have been more than accommodating of your inquiries. We're pretty far out from town, and we don't get many visitors. If that lady you're looking for had been this way, we would have noticed."

"How long ago did your wife run off?"

"That isn't any of your business. I bet you could get your answers in town. I'm going to have to ask you to leave."

"Thank you for the coffee."

Laura Lee heard footsteps and the door opening and then closing. She didn't come out of hiding for a long while. When she finally did, she couldn't stop shaking. Sharon hugged her and had her sit in a chair.

Tears filled her eyes as she glanced at Sharon and then Gideon. "I'm so sorry I brought that man to your door. I'm leaving in the morning. We'll all be safer. If a Pinkerton is looking for me than he thinks I committed a crime. My best bet is to leave while I know where he is."

"Where will you go, dear?" Sharon asked as she clasped and unclasped her hands.

"I'm going to backtrack then head west. If I'm lucky I'll end up on a ranch with a family I know. If not, there must be plenty of new towns cropping up. I know I'll be fine."

Gideon gave her a gentle smile. "God will be with you."

"Yes, He will. I'll be just fine, really. I'll need to take a few supplies with me..."

"Of course," Gideon agreed. "I'll start gathering what you'll need. I can take you south for a few hours. It'll give you a good head start."

"Thank you, Gideon." She glanced at Sharon. "All of you have been so very kind to me."

The next morning before dawn Laura Lee gave Sharon and Felix hugs goodbye. Sharon had clung to her, but Gideon told her they had to go.

He put a backpack on her. It was heavy but not too heavy. Then he mounted his horse, Tulip, and pulled her up behind him. Laura Lee wrapped her arms around his waist, and they started off.

The day had started with a slight chill in the air, but it grew warmer as they went. Finally, they came to a place near the forest where a well-marked trail began.

They both got down.

"I've been on that trail. It's easy enough. I added a gun to your pack. I hope you don't need it but just in case you run into wolves again..." He smiled while staring into her eyes. "My mother had you pegged as my next wife. If it had been another time... If I knew whether I'm married or not... But I couldn't do that to you no matter how much I enjoy your company."

Grinning at him she gave him a big hug. "Another time. I'm pleased I have a good friend in you. Take care of Felix, he so wants to be just like you." After a long look she turned and walked into the forest.

Chapter Ten

C aden leaned against a giant tree waiting for Laura Lee to walk closer. He'd been so concerned about her and while he had worried, it appeared she'd found herself a protector. His fists clenched and unclenched, and he tried to tamper down his anger. He didn't like being played for a fool and that was all she'd done; telling him lies upon lies.

"Sweet parting scene back there," he drawled. She jumped, and he enjoyed it. He enjoyed the terror-stricken expression on her face.

"Caden, I'm so glad to see you." She held her hand to her heart.

"You don't look like a nun in those boy clothes."

Her head dipped and she stared at the ground. Finally, she lifted her gaze to his and sighed.

"There is so much I need to tell you, Caden. When I'm done and you want to leave me here, I'll understand. I don't like lies, yet all I did was lie." She sounded contrite, but he reminded himself harshly that she couldn't be trusted.

"I know all about your lies. Pastor Mellon came to see me and my pa. His worry trumped his promise to you. I know you're not a nun, and I also know you're part of the Bannock Gang."

She walked away from him down the trail. His legs were longer, and he easily caught up.

"Nothing to say?"

"My last name is Bannock, but I never did anything illegal. There's a Pinkerton on my trail, and I don't know what he wants except he probably thinks like you, that I'm part of the gang. My part was I lived in the same house as my brother." Her head remained bowed as she spoke. "It hurts that you're so angry with me. I did think we were friends." She didn't so much glance at him the whole time.

It'd hurt him too. He'd thought they were friends. He really was mad, though, because of the man who had just dropped her off.

"Who was that man that gave you a ride?"

"I'd found these clothes in my travels north, and I hoped to sleep in the barn, but he saw me and brought me to the house. I was relieved to see he lived there with his mother and son. I just couldn't sleep in another tree while wolves circled below me."

Caden froze. "You had a run-in with wolves? You slept in a tree?"

"Yes, I did. I tied myself high enough on a sturdy branch. God must have been watching over me."

"I already know you aren't a nun, so you don't have to keep bringing God into the conversation." His voice grew louder.

"God is part of me, part of my life, and He always has been. I'm sorry I lied. Now everything I say is suspect."

"Let's keep walking, then we can rest and eat something."

"I have food to share," she offered.

He didn't answer her. There wasn't much to say. He needed to get ahold of himself. What was he supposed to think? He'd had feelings for her when she was a nun and that had made him feel all kinds of guilty. Learning she wasn't a nun was a shock... and a relief. Seeing her with that man had lit his anger. Was this jealousy? If so, he was doomed; he wouldn't be able to walk away from her.

Walking in silence had her on edge. She'd never met angry Caden before and she didn't like this side of him. His anger was understandable. If only she knew what she could do about it. They stopped and in the middle of the forest was a makeshift table and two crates.

"Why would a table be here?" she asked.

He lifted his left shoulder. "Maybe this is someone's favorite spot."

"It is beautiful under the trees with a view of the flowered meadow." She took off her pack and rummaged for food. "I have fresh muffins and cooked bacon. I have plenty." She sat on a crate and put her food out on the table. It hurt that he didn't turn toward her. He continued to stare at the meadow.

"I left Langford because I saw my brother and he saw me," she explained. "The evil grin he gave me scared me. Back home, he said if I left, he'd kill me and that smile was a sign he meant to keep his promise. Maybe my brother convinced that Pinkerton I had a part in the robberies. It makes me so queasy thinking about it. I had to hide from the Pinkerton. He was at the Strong farm yesterday looking for me. They have part of the gang in jail. I just don't understand." Her voice quivered but there was no help for it. Fear engulfed her.

Caden turned and stared. "I'll keep you safe. Don't worry so much."

If his words were meant to comfort her, they didn't. His voice was hard. How she wanted to ask but she didn't dare ask.

Caden finally sat, and they ate. They both avoided looking at the other.

"Caden I would ask for your forgiveness, but it wouldn't be right. I had a lengthy conversation with the pastor. I asked him if God forgave me for my lies. He told me yes to some but there wasn't forgiveness for something I knowingly lied about. When I was finished being a nun I could ask for forgiveness. I don't know what will happen. I might have to run again, and I might need to turn into a nun again. It's a heavy sin to carry."

He rubbed the back of his neck. "It's hard to swallow your whole pack of lies. I'm trying to understand, and I think I do but something inside doesn't completely trust you."

Her heart ached fiercely. "I understand. Where should I go? I thought north to be a safe bet, but it wasn't. I don't know what to do. Is there anywhere Ed won't find me? If not him then his gang will surely pursue me."

"You didn't marry one of them, did you?"

She took a deep breath and shook her head. "Marriage isn't what they had in mind. Ed made promises to the gang, and he couldn't make good on his promises when I escaped."

"You must have been frightened," Caden murmured.

"All the time. The walls were thin enough. I heard Ed explain he was going to shackle me so I wouldn't be able to get away."

"It's hard to believe all the things you've been through."

"You think I'm lying about everything?"

"No, I believe you. I guess I should have said it's beyond comprehension how a brother could do that to his sister." He reached across the table and covered her hand with his.

A glimmer of hope blossomed inside her. She wasn't fool enough to think Caden could come to care for her, but perhaps they could be friends again. When they finished eating, she packed everything up and put it in her knapsack.

"If that's heavy I could carry it or put some of your things in my bag," he offered.

"I'm fine. I'll let you know if it gets to be too much." Happiness began to bubble up, but she quickly tampered it down. He was just being a gentleman.

Chapter Eleven

They took a couple twists and turns away from the trail and came out at a small shack.

"I was wondering where your horse was," she remarked.

"I wasn't sure how dense the woods were. He was happy enough to stay here." They walked to the corral. "This is Rumble. Rumble this is Laura Lee." The smile on her face warmed him.

"The place isn't much, but it's better than sleeping in a tree," he teased.

She chuckled, and the sound boosted his mood further.

When she opened the door, something—possibly several somethings—scurried in the shadows.

"Mice?" she asked.

"That would be my guess. The place looks to be in good shape otherwise."

She set her pack down and grabbed the broom that was leaning against the wall. She stepped to where the sounds had come from and swept the broom under a chair covered with a dusty quilt. Something shuffled out into the open. The ringed tail and face mask allowed quick identification of the intruder. Quickly she backed away and then ran behind Caden.

"It's just a racoon," he told her, chuckling. He took the broom and shooed the animal out the front door. "There, that's taken care of." He set the broom back where it was.

"I'm not usually so skittish." Her blush amused him.

"I wouldn't think so. You did sleep in a tree with wolves underneath."

"That is true." Her eyes widened.

"Hey, I know that." He gentled his voice. She'd been through enough already.

"What's the plan?" She looked at him with confidence in her eyes. She was counting on him.

"As soon as I come up with one, I'll let you know. You'd be safe at the ranch, or I could take you to a different town and get you a place to live."

"You wouldn't stay there very long."

"I have a herd of cattle I can't be away from for too long. I think we need to think it over." He got busy building a fire while she put two chairs at the kitchen table. "I have food in my pack too."

"Let's eat mine for now."

He nodded then watched her graceful movements, frowning at the way the trousers revealed so much even while covering most of her legs. He couldn't take her home wearing those clothes. He didn't want any man staring at her, not even his brothers.

"You'll need to put your nun clothes on tomorrow. Wherever we decide to go, people just don't cotton to a female dressed like a man."

Her face turned red, and she quickly sat down at the table. "I have a dress in my pack. I'll hang it up so hopefully some of the wrinkles will fall out before I put it on. The Strong family was very good to me."

"Did that man Gideon have a hard time letting you go?" He sat across from her to see her reaction. He expected her to blush again, but she took a bite of her biscuit and seemed to be thinking about her answer.

"His mother had the hardest time. She thought I'd be a perfect wife for Gideon. Gideon liked me, and he was kind. We became friends, that's all."

"Was he immune to your feminine wiles?" he teased.

"I wouldn't even know where to start with that. I was sheltered growing up. I had a few friends, but my brother Ed was my best friend. When his gang moved in, I was in constant fear. They stared at me and said things I know shouldn't be said to a proper woman. I didn't know what they meant a lot of the time, but I knew from the tone of their voices none of it was good. I tried to be as invisible as I could. I stupidly thought Ed would put a stop to all the nonsense. He didn't. After I left, I pretended to be a nun, and I never glanced at another man if I could help it. You were my only male friend." She sighed and looked into his eyes. "It was confusing being your friend. I always felt warm and safe when you were near. I looked forward to seeing you and only you. What that means I have no idea. You were on my mind a lot." She stood and gazed out the window.

She was too naive to purposely lie for gain. He couldn't be angry she had masqueraded as a nun. She wasn't trying to make a fool out of anyone. It must have been scary to have to watch her every move and constantly look over her shoulder.

"I suppose you felt you were being hunted."

She turned to him. "That is exactly how I felt. I didn't dare tell anyone except for Pastor Mellon. But it doesn't change anything. The Bannock Gang will forever look for me."

Her sad eyes got to him.

"We'll go back to the ranch tomorrow. I can protect you there. The thought of you being in another town all alone is hard to fathom. I wouldn't feel I could leave you."

"Are you sure? I don't want anything to happen to your family because of me."

He stood, walked to her, and took her hands in his. "Trust me."

She nodded. They stood gazing at each other for a long moment before she pulled away.

"I think I'm going to try to get a good night's sleep." Laura Lee walked to the bed and looked under it first, then she pulled the quilt off and it must have been clean enough. She got into bed, clothes and all.

Caden sat before the hearth and watched the fiery red flames. She'd had a much more sheltered life than he'd imagined. It would be best to let her be. She should be able to go to barn dances or have someone court her. She hadn't had an opportunity to live yet. It wasn't going to be easy for him, but it was the best thing for her.

He unrolled his bedding and hunkered down in front of the fire, his gun within reach. Sleep didn't come easily.

Chapter Twelve

"How much longer?" Laura Lee asked.

"Not much. I'll stop soon so you can change into your dress."

"It'll be nice to get off Rumble." Saddle sore didn't even come close to an explanation of how her body hurt. Riding wasn't something she was used to. It was nice holding on to Caden, but it was becoming too nice. Over and over, she reminded herself that he was a good friend and that was all. He was her best friend but words like marriage and babies floated through her mind. It wouldn't be a good path. It was a path to heartbreak, and she wasn't about to go there.

After another half hour or so, Caden pulled up on the reins and brought Rumble to a stop. He jumped down and held out his arms to her. She slid into them, and once her feet hit the ground, she stepped away. After lifting her carefully folded dress from her pack she looked around for the best place to change.

There was a spot where bushes would give her full coverage. Dashing behind them she quickly switched clothing. It felt nice to wear a regular dress again. She removed her hairpins, let her hair fall around her shoulders and then twisted it back up into a fresh bun. After making sure the hairpins were secure, she left the bushes.

Caden whistled long and low. "You look beautiful. That dress suits you."

She blushed and dropped her gaze to the ground.

"Is something wrong?" Caden asked.

She shook her head.

"Did I do something wrong? Why won't you look at me?"

She met his worried stare. "No one has ever called me beautiful before, and I don't know how to react. Do I simply say thank you? Or do I compliment you back? I'm so awkward."

"You don't have to say anything. I didn't mean to embarrass you. You might want to get used to compliments, though. You are quite fetching." He grinned.

"I'm not sure about riding a horse with this dress on."

"You won't have to. We're about five minutes away from the ranch house. We'll walk."

"Oh, good." Her shoulders tensed.

"It'll be just fine. We'll go in the back door and make sure no one who shouldn't be there is in the house."

"Like the Pinkerton or the sheriff?"

He nodded. "Yes, to both. Come on." He offered his hand and she seemed hesitant, but she took it.

"Oh my! Look who is home!" Nessa gave them a big smile. "Your pa's been fretting but don't tell him I told you."

"Are there any lawmen around?" he asked.

"Gracious, no. Pierce isn't allowing them on the property. Go sit down and I'll bring you coffee." She shooed them away.

Caden dropped Laura Lee's hand and pushed the door open. They walked into the main area of the house. Cait, Myles' wife and Erieann, Aiden's wife sat on the sofa talking. They both turned their heads in their direction.

Cait hopped up. "I'm so glad you found her!"

"Are you all right?" Erieann asked.

"I'm fine," Laura Lee said in a quiet voice.

Cait took her by the hand and led her to a seat on the couch.

Laura Lee was just settling in when Eion entered the room. He beckoned to her, and she went to him. He grabbed her up into a bear hug. He held her head against his shoulder and rocked them back and forth. Then he stepped back and cradled her face in his hands.

"You're safe here. I can't fathom what your life has been like." He smiled and kissed her on the forehead. Eion turned and nodded at Caden. "You did a fine job, son."

Laura Lee sat on the couch between Erieann and Cait. It felt strange yet wonderful having everyone welcome her back. It was almost as if this was her home. The glorious warmth dumbfounded her. This was a happy family.

"You look good in a dress," Cait commented.

"I bet it's cooler than the wool you wore," Erieann added.

"I met a nice family, and I was given this dress." She smiled then frowned as troubled thoughts resurfaced. "I don't want to put any of you in danger. My brother swore to kill me, and now there is a Pinkerton trying to find me. It's probably best I don't stay long."

Caden sat in an upholstered chair directly in front of her. He frowned. "I told you I'd protect you, and I meant it. You are staying until we get this all figured out."

She swallowed hard. "You plan on telling me what to do?" She kept her voice as even as she could.

"Yes."

"Caden, I do appreciate all you have done for me but I'm a woman grown. Staying here would be the smart thing to do, but I don't need you to control my life."

Erieann clapped. "Laura Lee is right. You get further explaining rather than telling. No one likes orders."

Caden glanced at his father, who raised a shoulder and let it drop.

"Laura Lee, I didn't mean it that way. I know that's how I said it, but I know you have a mind of your own. I apologize." An easy grin spread across his face.

His grin warmed her, and she smiled back. "I'm sorry too. I've been living on edge, and I'm taking it out on you."

"You two sound like an old married couple," Cait said with a laugh.

Laura Lee locked gazes with Caden. His expression revealed nothing. What was he thinking? Her breath backed up in her chest. He finally looked away.

"Were people mad when they found out I'm not a nun?" It was a question she needed to ask but didn't really want the answer.

"I'd say everyone was surprised," Eion stated. "Probably about a seventy, thirty split."

"That many think I did the wrong thing?" She released a sigh. "I thought it would be that way."

"No, seventy percent were in your favor. Mallory was surprised but understood." Eion paused. "Donna wants your head on a spike."

"Oh my! She really said spike?" Her heart dropped.

"No." Cait took her hand. "She said platter, not spike. She'll get over it. She thought you two were close, and perhaps she feels a bit betrayed. I'd just give it some time."

"I can understand. So, everyone knows now?"

Cait gave her hand a squeeze. "Apparently." Then she let go of her hand.

She'd fight to get all her friends back and change the opinion of the naysayers. It would have to wait until she was safe, though. How long would that be?

Chapter Thirteen

"It's about time you pulled your weight around here," Nolan remarked.

"I was gone less than three days. Couldn't handle the cows on your own?" Caden teased.

"One was bogged down in the mud, and I swear it kept mooing your name." Nolan chuckled. "It took almost half a day to get her out and that was with Mack helping me."

"Mud? It hasn't rained in forever."

"We have an underground spring running along the edge of the pasture. All these years and no one knew."

"Did you follow it to its origin?"

Nolan stared at him. "And when would I have had time to do that with having to do everything?"

"You don't have so much to do. We have ranch hands. How long did you try to pull the cow out of the mud before you sought help?" Caden asked.

"A few hours at the most," Nolan said his voice sounding testy.

Caden laughed hard until Nolan joined in.

"What's the plan for the little filly of yours?" Nolan asked as they walked their horses across the pasture.

"If by 'little filly' you mean Laura Lee, why would I have a plan other than to protect her?" There were so many plans that might not come to fruition that he didn't want to discuss them. Plans of courting, really getting to know her.

"I see how you two look at each other when you think no one is watching."

"We don't stare in each other's eyes." Caden frowned.

"I mean how you go all moon-eyed when you think she's not looking and how she looks the same when she sees you."

"I'm just a friend is all. She's got too much on her plate to think of romantic thoughts," Caden insisted.

"Just what I thought," Nolan called over his shoulder as he rode faster.

Did she really look at him that way? Maybe he could catch her looking. Nolan wasn't the most reliable source of information. He thought of love as a game. He jerked to a stop in his tracks. Love? Love wasn't in his plans for a long, long time. He had too much to do with the cattle breeding program. He didn't have time for a wife or family. He was getting way ahead of himself, and he needed to reel his thoughts back in. He hardly knew Laura Lee and she'd never mentioned she even liked him in a special way.

"I'm sorry I slept so late," Laura Lee apologized as she approached the dining table and sat down.

"No problem," Eion said. "Help yourself to some coffee, and I'm sure Nessa or Mary Jane will be here with your breakfast soon. I just received good news from Sheriff Stilton. The Bannock Gang is all locked up."

"All of them?" She widened her eyes. "Are you sure?"

"The sheriff was confident, but he needs you to go to the jailhouse to identify them. Also, you can let him know if he's missing anyone."

Nessa came in from the kitchen with a plate of eggs and pancakes. She set the plate down in front of Laura Lee. "Are you feeling all right?"

"Laura Lee?" Eion tried to get her attention.

"Yes, I'm dizzy is all. I'll be fine."

"You're so pale!" Nessa exclaimed.

"Maybe if I eat something..." Her stomach churned at the thought of going to the jailhouse. She shoved her plate away. "Actually, I need some fresh air. If you'll excuse me?" Her legs wobbled a bit, but she made it to the door. Before she could lift the latch, it opened. Caden stood in the doorway.

"You don't look so good."

She maneuvered around him and hurried outside. She made it to the woods before she was sick. It hurt her empty stomach to keep retching. Finally, she wiped her mouth off with her handkerchief and sat against a tree a few yards upwind from where she'd been sick.

It was as though all her troubles came pouring over her at the same time. Fatigue encompassed her. There was no way she could go and identify those men. She just couldn't.

"Do you want me to help you up or do you need a few minutes?" Caden asked.

"I'm a bit shaky at the moment."

"Are you with child?"

Her jaw dropped before she quickly snapped it closed. "What are you talking about?"

"I don't know I suppose, and if I insulted you, I'm sorry."

Her face heated. "You believed... I thought we were friends." She sighed and shook her head. "Thinking about identifying my brother and his gang has made me sick. I don't feel I can do it. I don't want to see any of them again. They are mean and nasty and had me living in fear." She swallowed hard trying to keep her tears at bay. Turning her head so he wouldn't see, tears rolled down her face.

He considered her as a woman of loose morals. What else could go wrong? Her heart felt so battered, and not one solution came to mind. She'd finally reached her breaking point.

Chapter Fourteen

C aden was just about to put his arm around her, to comfort her when they spotted Pierce and the Pinkerton riding up. Laura Lee stiffened and reached for his hand. She shook badly.

They waited sitting under the tree for the two men to reach them.

"I'm Johnson Lovett and I'm here to apprehend this woman you know as Laura Lee Bannock."

She gasped.

"What do you mean known as?" Caden demanded as he stood.

"Her real name is Sammy Burns. Sometimes she goes by Sammy Jo." The Pinkerton smiled.

Caden turned and helped Laura Lee stand. He'd never seen such a look of confusion on anyone's face before.

"I'm who?" she asked, her voice cracking. She swayed and Caden put his arm around her waist and held her close. "I don't know that name Mr. Lovett. Why would you think I'm this woman?"

"So coy, Mrs. Burns." He shook his head. "You escaped your hanging. I've been trailing you for almost a year now."

"I'm taking Laura Lee inside." Caden started to walk her toward the house.

"I'm coming too. She can say her goodbyes before I shackle her and take her in."

"Now hold on." Pierce stepped in front of the Pinkerton.

Caden swung Laura Lee into his arms and carried her inside. If he could take her and hide her, he would. There was no doubt Johnson Lovett would follow.

Eion stood right up and eyed the Pinkerton. "A second Pinkerton? I told the first one, a John Sanders, I believe, to stay off my property."

"Sanders is off the case. I'm on your property to collect that woman." He pointed at Laura Lee. "She's wanted for murder. Sammy Jo Burns has been wanted for over a year. She escaped one hanging but she wouldn't escape her fate again." Johnson had a great poker face, but his voice was full of excitement.

"Will you stop saying that? It's not me," Laura Lee insisted.

Caden led her to the couch and sat with her. Just being close to him was comforting but if the Pinkerton decided to take her there wasn't a thing Caden could do.

"If you're looking for this Sammy Jo why did you ask people if they've seen a Laura Lee?" She gave him her best stare.

"You'd changed your name along the way. Very clever with the nun outfit. It took me a while to find you again." He lifted his shoulders and let them drop. "But here we are."

"My brother is the leader of the Bannock Gang. I thought you were trailing me because of that."

"Nice try. You know, the sister died." The Pinkerton smirked.

"How did she—? Wait." What sister was he talking about? Not Sister Teresa? "What sister?"

"Nice try," sneered Lovett Johnson. "Bannock's sister."

"Who?" Laura Lee frowned. Nothing about this was making sense. "Are you saying you think I stole a dead woman's name?" Her heart ached. No matter what she said he had some convoluted answer.

"It's the oldest trick there is, taking a dead person's name. Laura Lee was in love with one of the gang, and he didn't want her. She threw herself over a cliff."

Laura Lee gasped. "This stops right now. There is no way I'd ever love anyone in that gang, and that includes my brother. My brother Ed rode out one day and two weeks later he returned with five men and a whole lot of money. I carried a gun and a knife on me because I was terrified of them. I barricaded myself in my room at night. I even nailed boards over my window. One night I heard their vile plans for me, and I pried the wood off the window and snuck out. My name was Laura Lee then and it still is my name." She shifted so she was a bit closer to Caden.

Eion cleared his throat. "I'd like to see the wanted poster."

Johnson grumbled but pulled a piece of paper from his inside jacket pocket. "Here it is. We need to get going."

"Wait until I've looked this over," Eion grouched. "Explain to me how this is Laura Lee? The picture looks nothing like her, and the description is for a much older woman." He cleared his throat. "And there seems to be a height difference."

"It's her all right," snarled Johnson. "I can just tell. Now you'll have to move along. I'm on official business." He took a step toward her with shackles in his hands.

Once he had her, he'd never let her go. He'd make sure she was hanged and call it a day.

With Mack on one side and Pierce on the other they both drew their guns. Eion took Johnson's gun and snatched the shackles from his grasp. Then he used them to shackle the Pinkerton's hands behind his back.

"Pierce, have someone get the sheriff."

"Will do, Boss." Pierce left the house.

"I'll take you upstairs Laura Lee," Caden told her. She nodded feeling so grateful. The McKeegans were brave and kind. Glancing over her shoulder she frowned at the Pinkerton. He gave her a look of evil. A chill ran up her spine, and she hurried up the stairs. What if Sheriff Stilton sided with Johnson Lovett?

"Stay up here. You'll be safe," Caden tried to reassure her.

"Can't you stay with me?"

He pulled her close and held her. "I'll be right downstairs. I need to know you'll stay up here. I don't want to get distracted because I'm worrying about you. Please?" He pulled back and they stared at each other.

She nodded. "I'll stay but if things sound like I'm going to be arrested, I'm going out the window."

His lips twitched. "Let's hope it doesn't come to that."

Johnson refused to talk until the sheriff arrived. Caden wanted to pace, it was hard sitting, watching him. The wanted poster was ridiculous! Finally, when he thought he couldn't take much more, Pierce walked in with the sheriff right behind him.

Sheriff Stilton took one look at the tied up man and frowned. "You have yourself a bit of a problem." He shook his head. "Johnson Lovett, I already told you there is no Sammy Burns around here."

"Stilton, you just didn't look but that's what I get paid to do. Laura Lee is most certainly Sammy Burns. You just aren't looking hard enough or maybe since one of the McKeegans is sweet on her, you refuse to look!"

"Now, see here Lovett, this is my town, and I don't appreciate you putting your nose in other people's business. Laura Lee did pretend to be a nun, but that's not against the law. It was right smart of her to use such a disguise. Her brother is ruthless. I have my hands full with the Bannock Gang in my jail. I don't need your Sammy Burns nonsense."

Johnson shook his head. "You have no reason to hold me here. I know people."

Stilton laughed. "We all know people. And I know people who say you aren't a Pinkerton. This is how this is going to go, you will leave this ranch and never set foot on it again. You understand me?"

Johnson's face turned red. "I hear you."

"By the way, Sammy Jo Burns was found in Texas. Maybe you should head south. Pierce, would you mind escorting this... this... well, Mr. Lovett off the ranch? I'd like to speak with the McKeegans."

Pierce was quick getting the pretend Pinkerton out of the house.

When things settled and a bit of peace fell over them, Sheriff Stilton addressed Eion. "We *do* have a little problem. Ed Bannock claims his sister is the brains behind all the heists. I don't believe a word of it, but a judge might. My advice is for her to go to town, visit the orphanage, attend church and other things women do in town. The more she is seen, the less suspicious she appears. One other thing, Sammy Jo Burns isn't in Texas that I know of. I made that part up. Can't stand that Lovett. If you need anything else let me know." He shook hands with Eion and Caden before he left.

"Looks like you need to escort Laura Lee to town," Eion said as he patted Caden on the back.

Chapter Fifteen

"You don't need to be nervous," Caden told her.

"Tell me you wouldn't be nervous to go to a dance where everyone will stare at you."

Caden chuckled. "I always get stared at by the females."

Laura Lee shook her head. She didn't bother trying to hide her grin. The plan was for the family to walk into the barn together. *A show of solidarity* Eion had said.

She slid her hands down the front of her gown making sure the wrinkles were smoothed out. The new dress was a gift from the McKeegan women. It was made from a deep green calico material and trimmed all in lace. Not just the collar, her sleeves and hem were trimmed too. The three generous women had already donated a few of their dresses to her but this was so special. It made her feel pretty.

"There's no need to fuss; you look lovely," Caden told her.

"Thank you. I'm afraid but I know afterward I can ask God's forgiveness for pretending to be a nun. I told so many lies." Her heart dropped.

"Hey, stand tall and smile. I'll stay by your side."

"You don't have to. I bet there are plenty of ladies you'd like to dance with."

He took her hand and gave it a quick squeeze before letting it go. "I don't mind."

She hid a chuckle behind a cough. He didn't dance once at the last dance. He probably hated dancing.

"I appreciate your sacrifice."

"Ready?"

The McKeegans walked into the Orphanage and continued to the ballroom. She stood tall and smiled as they entered. Was it her imagination or did everyone get louder? Her bottom lip quivered. Caden immediately put his hand on the small of her back. It was as though he gave her a bit of his courage.

"Would you like some punch?" Caden asked.

"Which bowl are you getting it from?"

He laughed. "You don't think anyone really spikes that punch bowl, do you?"

"Of course, they do. I stood guard at the last dance."

"Don't you think more men would be drinking punch out of that bowl?"

She furrowed her brow. "That is a very interesting observation, Caden. Why didn't you say something at the last dance?"

"You were a nun."

"Enough said." She sighed. "People are staring."

"Laura Lee, may I have this dance?" Eion stood in front of her offering his arm.

"Of course. I'd be honored." She took his arm and allowed him to lead her to the dance floor. "I'm not much of a dancer," she whispered to Eion.

"Just follow me and smile. We wouldn't want the community to think I'm stepping on your toes."

She chuckled. "Thank you. I know you're showing your approval of me, and it means more than I can say."

"I happen to like you. You have gumption and I don't think your acts of kindness came about because you were dressed as a nun."

Her face heated. "Thank you."

The dance ended and Eion escorted her back to the McKeegan family. The fear inside her was dissipating. Perhaps she'd enjoy herself after all.

Caden brought her punch, and they exchanged grins. A lot of people were on the dance floor once the square dancing started. There were partners who looked as though they square danced daily and others who were just beginning.

Loud talking and guffawing grew exceptionally loud at the front door. People mostly looked as though they were ignoring the ruckus. Several men stood at the entrance to the ballroom. She glanced at the group and cringed. There stood Slim Barker, a sometime member of her brother's gang.

Her heartbeat felt erratic as fear filled her. She quickly turned her back on the men. Slim might not even know she was here.

"I'm going to see what's going on," Caden announced.

She shot out her hand and grabbed his arm. "They have guns," she managed to say. Her throat felt as though it was narrowing. "It's Ed's friend. I don't know the others but Slim is dangerous."

Guns weren't allowed at the dance and most abided by the rule. Caden was keenly aware of his and everyone else's disadvantage. He quickly scanned the crowd for the sheriff, but he didn't see him. The dances were usually a combined fund raiser for the orphanage and the church. No one thought there'd be trouble.

The men started walking in. They were glassy eyed and one staggered. Drunk no doubt.

The McKeegan men formed a wall in front of their women. They'd gladly take a bullet to protect what was theirs.

"I have a gun in my boot," Myles whispered.

"So do I," Nolan said.

The rest nodded. Caden was the only one who didn't have a weapon. He wouldn't be able to protect anyone. He might as well go sit with the women. What a fool, why hadn't he thought to put a gun in his boot?

A shot rang out.

Chapter Sixteen

One of the ruffians shot into the air. "Listen up!" Laura Lee recognized Slim's voice. "Take your valuables out and be ready to drop them into the bag my partners will be coming around with. After that we'll be takin' Laura Lee Bannock off your hands."

Maybe if she made her way to the door and gave herself up, they'd just go. It was the only way to keep everyone safe.

The McKeegan men slowly, one by one retrieved their firearms. There were too many people between them and the gang. Someone was going to get hurt. This was her responsibility. Many of the people at the dance had been more than kind to her.

She stood. Cait tried to pull her back down, but Laura Lee was able to shake Cait off and instead of walking through the wall of protectors she made her way around them before they could stop her.

"Slim! Slim Barker! I believe you're looking for me?" Slim's grin turned her stomach. She could hear Caden asking her what she was doing.

After pushing her way to the door, she glanced at Slim. "Let's go," she said. She walked out into the night.

Her life was forfeited, but it was all she could do to keep everyone alive. "Where's Ed?"

"Around. There was a jail break a few minutes ago," Slim answered as he painfully gripped her arm and led her to his horse. "It was a stroke of luck I spotted you going into the dance. Ed is going to be so happy to see you."

He tossed her up, onto his horse and settled in behind her. "Don't make me tie you."

A sense of defeat surrounded her. He'd shoot her in the back if she tried to run. It might be a quicker less painful death than her brother planned. Her faith was strong but doubt crept in. The Lord was always with her, both in life and in death. It was the only hope she had to cling to.

"Though I walk through the valley of the shadow of death," she mouthed silently, "I will fear no evil. For thou art with me..."

She didn't remember it being so cold.

The McKeegan men raced out the back door. Caden raced to the first wagon he saw, and sure enough there was a rifle under the front bench. He grabbed it and raced after his brothers.

They were running along the back of the town buildings until they caught sight of the gang. Their horses were pulling this way and that as though they wanted to turn back. The McKeegans split up, moving along different alleys toward the road.

Caden ducked down. The horse in front of him was the horse Laura Lee and her captor sat. The horses continued to dance.

"Put down your guns! You're surrounded." It sounded like a woman.

A shot was fired, and chaos began. Caden watched as Slim pistol-whipped Laura Lee and allowed her to fall to the ground. Blood flowed from her head and she was in danger of being stepped on by one of the horses.

"Cover me," he shouted to Aiden. Then Caden crouched low. The outlaws seemed to be looking toward the front. The horses raced forward and dust flew everywhere making it hard to see. Caden reached Laura Lee and picked her up.

A few shots came their way, but Aiden covered them until he returned to the alley. Then Aiden ran for the back, probably trying to get ahead of the gang.

There was more gunfire and Caden placed Laura Lee on the ground, covering her with his body.

"Well, well here she is."

Caden looked up and stared at Ed Bannock. "Leave while you still can," Caden growled.

The next thing he knew Ed was falling. Quickly Caden scooped up Laura Lee and ran back down the alley. There were several oil lamps lit by a group of wagons. He hurried toward them and placed Laura Lee on a blanket on the ground. There were several townspeople receiving care from the doctor and a few of the women attending the wounded.

"Was she shot?" the doctor asked.

"No, she was hit pretty hard with a gun. She fell to the ground after that. She hasn't opened her eyes."

Mallory came running over with a clean wet cloth. "Let me clean off the blood so we can see how bad it is."

He would swear it was the first time he'd taken a breath since he saw her get hit. Caden was on his knees holding Laura Lee's head still, while Mallory cleaned the wound.

"Head wounds bleed a lot, Caden," Mallory explained.

"Does she need to be stitched?" The doctor shouted over to Mallory.

"No, I'm just going to bandage her. She still hasn't come to."

"Don't let anyone move her. I'll be there when I can, though there isn't much I can do."

Mallory nodded and glanced at Caden.

"I heard it all. Is she dying?" His heart dropped as anger and despair consumed him.

"No, she'll open her eyes when she's ready. I know it's hard to watch her like this, but that's all we can do. I can go get one of your brothers."

"They'll be by this way, I'm sure. Thanks Mallory. It looks like there are more and more people coming to help."

"Mr. Ryder is bringing every blanket he has. I'll be back to check on her."

Caden nodded. He kept his gaze on Laura Lee. His feelings for her were deeper than he'd realized. If she died, he'd never get a chance to tell her how much she meant to him. They'd hardly gotten to know one another, but he liked everything about her so far. If only he could have the chance to get to know her better.

Nolan was right, he'd been mooning over Laura Lee ever since he first caught sight of her.

Reaching out, Caden brushed the hair off her forehead. Her face was so white, and she was so still. She was the most beautiful woman he'd ever seen. If only he could gaze into her blue eyes.

Chapter Seventeen

3 weeks later

Laura Lee quickly closed the door behind her and locked it. She usually had an open door to all but today she just couldn't. She was glad for the windowless room. Watching would be unbearable. Thinking about it was destroying. She might have been afraid of her brother but watching him hang was something she refused to do.

Working at the orphanage the last two weeks had given her clarity. This town was her home now, and she intended to stay. She'd been on the receiving end of some very disapproving stares, but hopefully they would go away with time.

She'd spent plenty of afternoons in the church praying. First for forgiveness. The Pastor had told her if she stopped lying about being a nun she could ask for God's forgiveness. The first few afternoons, she didn't feel it. The expected lightness in her soul didn't happen. Her burden hadn't felt lifted. That troubled her. The only thing she knew to do was pray. The fourth day while praying in the church, her heart expanded as it was filled with God's love and grace. In that moment she knew she was forgiven. It was one of the most profound moments in her life.

Walking by the gallows being built was torturous. Knowing about a hanging was awful but the fact that it was her brother... How was she going to get through? Although he'd been a monster to her, she still remembered how it had been when they were kids.

So much had changed.

A chill went through her. The hangings were probably starting. So many people had come to town to watch the *excitement*. She'd be safe but wishing death on someone wasn't something she could do. All she could do was pray for his soul. She bowed her head and prayed.

Caden hadn't planned to come to town, but he was worried about Laura Lee. Would she be in the crowd waiting? Pastor Mellon stood at the top of the gallows reading passages from the Bible aloud. The crowd was boisterous, and that bothered him. Death wasn't something to celebrate.

She wasn't there, and relief coursed through him. That was for the best. He hadn't seen her except right after she'd opened her eyes. She had been taken to her room at the orphanage to recover. He missed her. From what he'd heard she was back to teaching, but she was rarely seen in public these days. He was happy for her but not so happy for himself. Try as he might, he hadn't been able to come up with believable reasons to come to town and call at the orphanage. Nolan had suggested he stay away until all the talk stopped.

A loud gasp brought him out of his musing. It had begun. He didn't even look to see who went first. All he wanted was to see Laura Lee.

He walked into the orphanage and knocked on Laura Lee's door. He waited a minute. Where could she be? He took a step away when he heard a sob. He tried to open the door, but it was locked.

"Laura Lee, it's me honey. I thought you might need a hug." A hug? Had he lost all his good sense? What would she do with a hug? He sure was no good at this.

The door opened slowly. Laura Lee stepped away from it to allow him in. His heart wrenched; her eyes were puffy and red-rimmed. He didn't give it much thought before he went in and closed the door behind him.

He took her into his arms, tucked her head under his chin and held her tight as she sobbed.

"I'm getting your shirt all wet," she croaked after a while.

"It's fine. It's just a shirt. It's you I'm worried about."

She hugged him back tightly and wept harder. She sobbed for quite a while before she quieted. She let go of him and took a step back. Clasping her hands, she gazed at the floor.

"I'm sorry."

"Hey, look at me. You have nothing to be sorry about."

She glanced at him quickly before looking away. "He wasn't a good person. He robbed and killed people."

"He's your brother. Those connections run deep. I understand. I'm glad you didn't watch. It's morbid out there. People are clapping."

"It's big excitement for some. I prayed for his soul. I was going to go to church to pray but I didn't want to be around people."

"I'm sure your prayers were heard just the same. Are you planning to stay here or move back to your family home?"

She looked startled. "I hadn't given it any thought. I don't even know if the house is still standing."

"You know you can always come to the ranch to visit. I haven't seen you in two weeks."

She gave him a sad smile. "I know you're busy. Besides, I didn't want the gossip to start again."

"I understand," he commented.

"Speaking of gossip, you need to leave. Having the door closed with you in here isn't setting a good example for the children."

"You're right." He put his finger under her chin and lifted it until he could look into her eyes. "If you need anything, come to the ranch." He tried to determine what she was thinking, but she pasted on a smile he knew wasn't real. "I'll see you soon."

"Thank you."

Unsettled was how he felt. If she had given him the least amount of encouragement, he'd want to court her. But she didn't seem interested. Like she aways said they were friends.

Chapter Eighteen

T he house looked smaller than she remembered. She really hadn't been gone all that long, only a little over two years, but it still looked smaller. There was garbage everywhere, along with dirty discarded clothes. The US Marshalls had been through the house looking for stolen items and gold. They'd recovered some but not all.

Once she cleaned it and set it to rights, she'd be fine. She didn't have much money but if she could get the garden to grow, she'd get through the winter.

She had wanted to stay in Langford so badly, but it was just too difficult. Walking along the street to the general store, she'd sensed the stares, heard the whispers... And knowing her brother had died there... But worst of all, Caden seemed to have closed himself off to her.

Sighing, she shook her head to clear her thoughts.

She needed to check the root cellar. She had canned a lot of food before she'd had to run. It was probably all gone. The steps to the cellar were in her room under a rag carpet. Surprisingly it was still there. Maybe there was hope.

The rug wasn't heavy; it was dusty though. Dragging it outside was easy enough. She went back and pulled the hatch up, taking the time to light the oil lamp that hung under the opening. The musty smell assailed her as she went down the creaky stairs. The space was empty except for a crate of glass jars. At least she didn't have to carry and dump any rotted food.

She'd set snares and catch rabbits. That would give her plenty of meat. There was lots of time to get ready for the winter. Right now, she had a house to clean. She climbed up the ladder.

What would she need for tonight? After checking the oil lamps, she was grateful to have several that contained oil. She'd packed a bedroll so she had a place to sleep. Going outside, she located the bucket right next to the well. There'd be no wasted time hunting for it.

After she placed the bucket in the house, she went in search of firewood. Many tree trunks were lying around. It would take some effort to chop the wood into smaller pieces, but she was used to hard work. One thing at a time.

She chopped what she'd need for that evening and the next morning. Hopefully, there would be some gloves inside. Blisters were already forming.

It took a lot of hard work, but at last the kitchen and sitting room were clean. There was now a huge pile of junk in the yard. That would be burned another day.

Tomorrow the garden needed to be taken care of. From what she saw, it was just a big plot of weeds. She prayed she would find something edible in it. For now, she took a jar of jam, a big hunk of cheese, and some biscuits out of one of her bags. After taking just a small amount she put it up in a cupboard. If only Mama was here. It was so quiet. Something to get used to.

"What do you mean she left? Mallory, how long has she been gone?" Caden hadn't believed it when he'd heard Laura Lee had left. He still couldn't believe it even after seeing her empty room. Why hadn't she told him she was going? He'd thought, hoped... It didn't matter what he'd thought. She was gone.

"She's been gone for over a week and you are just now discovering it. Caden, if you really cared, you'd have stopped by before this." Mallory's voice was gentle, but her words stung.

It was never a thought she'd leave. She hadn't even said goodbye.

"Did she say where she was going?"

"She said, she was going home. That it was the one place she really fit in." Mallory released a sigh. "I'm sorry I shouldn't have snapped at you."

"I thought she needed time. I assumed between her brother's death and the town gossip she'd just stayed inside. I wanted to encourage her to go for a walk with me." His stomach churned and his heart felt empty. "Thanks, Mallory."

Still stunned, he made his way to his horse and started for home. What a fool. She left him. He should have checked on her. He wasn't any good at relationships. He stopped at the edge of Rosemary's Valley. One of the most lovely and majestic places on the ranch, it was named after his mother. Myles and

Cait had recently moved into the house they'd built on the other side of the valley.

His mother would have known what to do. She'd have some words of wisdom for him, spoken in an Irish brogue. He smiled, thoughts of his mother warming his otherwise devastated heart. He wished he didn't know what love was. Turning Rumble, he road for home.

When he got to the barn, he handed his reins to one of the men. He usually took care of his own horses, but he just wanted to be inside.

It was quiet in the house, an unusual occurrence. He put his gun belt and hat on the table near the door then sat in one of the chairs near the fireplace. What should he do?

"You're home," Nessa greeted him as she bustled out of the kitchen. I have meatloaf I can heat up for you if you like, and I just finished making a pot of coffee."

"Thanks, Nessa, that sounds good."

She gave him an inquiring look before she went back into the kitchen. He wasn't in the mood for questions. Where had Laura Lee lived before she ran away from her brother and his gang? He thought hard about it but had no recollection of her ever saying where she'd come from.

The sheriff! He was bound to know.

But she didn't want him to find her. She would have at least said goodbye if she'd wanted to stay in touch. They would have exchanged pleasantries about keeping in touch, and maybe they actually would have done so. None of that had happened. Not one word.

"Food is ready," Nessa announced.

He gave her a quick smile before he went to the table and sat at the place where his meal was waiting.

Aiden came from the den and took a seat across from Caden.

"Thanks Nessa," Aiden said with a grin as Nessa brought him a cup of coffee. None of them had to ask for much. Nessa seemed to know.

"Did you know Laura Lee was leaving town?" Caden asked.

Aiden frowned. "I haven't heard a thing about it. When did she leave?"

"Mallory didn't say exactly, but more than a week ago. She went back home." He stared at the table in front of him. "I don't even know where that is."

"I'm sorry, I know you two were friends."

Caden lifted his right shoulder then let it drop. "I *thought* we were. I stayed away too long. I'm no good with people who are upset. I didn't know what to say and I thought I'd give her some peace for a few weeks. I should have been a better friend to her."

"Don't be so hard on yourself. Pa might know where she's from. Mr. Rider is certain to know."

"I didn't think of Mr. Rider, but you're right! He's my best bet. He knows everything that goes on."

Aiden finished his coffee and stood. "I saw the way she looked at you. If I were you, I'd go get her."

"I'll give it some more thought. My heart has a big hole in it, and I need to figure a few things out."

His brother tilted his head and studied him for a moment. "Don't take too long figuring," he suggested.

Chapter Nineteen

One morning Laura Lee opened the door to go weed the garden as she did every morning. Mr. Beeves at the general store had told her he could take vegetables, fruits, and jams as trades.

"Oh, I didn't see you there." She stared down at a young woman who looked as though she hadn't bathed in a year. The woman was shivering. "Up you go, let's get you inside. I bet you're cold and hungry."

The woman nodded and slowly stood as though it was painful for her. Her troubles became obvious as her large belly showed. The poor thing was with child.

Laura Lee helped the woman inside and sat her in a chair next to the stove. Then she opened the stove door and added more wood. Next, she went into the spare room and took the quilt off the bed. She wrapped the woman in the quilt.

"There now, one problem solved." Laura Lee smiled. "I'll heat water for coffee, and I have fresh bread and jam I can spread on top."

The girl nodded eagerly.

"I'm Laura Lee Bannock. What's your name?"

"I'm Tierney." Her voice was lifeless and judging by the circles under her eyes, she was exhausted.

Laura Lee spread the raspberry jam on the bread in a thick layer. "I'll give you one slice and see how that goes. I wish I had some milk for you."

Tierney took the plate and stared at it for a moment. Then she took a small bite. The rest she shoved into her mouth. She looked at the floor sheepishly and finished chewing. "You must think I have no manners. I haven't eaten in two days."

"The coffee will be done soon. Do you mind if I ask why, you are outside without a coat or anything else?"

"I suppose you could say I ran away from home."

"You left your husband?"

Tierney slowly shook her head. "I'm not married. My ma and pa tell me every moment that I've shamed them. You wouldn't believe some of the words that came out of Pa's mouth. Nothing but filth."

"What about the baby's father?"

"I wish I had some tragic romantic story of love but it didn't happen that way. One of my pa's friends attacked me." Her head bowed.

"I'm so sorry that happened to you. People can be cruel in deed and word. From the bit you've told me you are not shameful."

Laura Lee pulled out two mugs and poured coffee into both. She took the empty plate from Tierney and handed her the coffee.

"I don't have sugar, sorry."

"That's just fine. Thank you for allowing me to warm by your stove. I'll need to be going. I like to try to find a place to sleep before it's dark." Tierney sighed.

"Where are you headed? Do you have family you can stay with?"

"No. My parents pinned all their hopes for the future on me, and I ruined everything. I'm sorry that sounds so bitter." Tears filled her eyes.

"Stay here for a few days at least. You'd be surprised how much difference rest and good food makes. I live here alone now."

Tierney looked around. "Only for a few days, though."

"Help yourself. I'm going to take care of the garden. Then I need to finish making dresses. Readymade dresses are selling well. Mr. Beeves at the general store is paying me a commission on each dress. I'm saving for a cow. Milk, butter, and cheese! I'm looking forward to it."

"I'm no good with a needle, but I could be of help in the garden," Tierney offered.

"Let's wait until tomorrow. You look like you need a bit of rest." Laura Lee gathered her bonnet, work gloves, and a basket. "Yell out the back door if you need me."

Tierney smiled at her. Walking toward the garden she couldn't shake the feeling something was off. Thinking over the whole morning and each word they'd said didn't help clear anything up. Besides, doing for others was a way to pay back all the blessings she'd been given.

There weren't many weeds. She tended the garden daily. It was watering all the plants that was the hard work. It would have been better planning to put the garden closer to the well.

Not too much longer and she'd have enough money for a cow. She had five dresses made and another almost finished. Then the long trek into town. Maybe one of these years she'd even be able to afford a horse.

The sun beat down on her, signaling it was time to go inside. She looked up at the white puffy clouds and smiled.

Thank You, Lord, for this beautiful day. Thank You for the many blessings You have bestowed upon me. I have a woman in my kitchen who could use a blessing, both her and the child she carries. Amen

After gathering everything up she went back inside. She was speechless to find Tierney wearing one of the dresses for the general store. And she was holding up another one.

Chapter Twenty

"Be careful not to get them dirty. I'm relying on the sale of each dress. That includes the one you have on."

Tierney dropped the dress onto the pile of nicely folded dresses.

"You must admit my dress is nothing but a rag. I thought I'd wear this one." She touched the skirt on the yellow gingham dress. "I think it suits me."

"I'm sorry but I can't afford to give away the dresses I've been making for sale. I came back home without any money and slowly I saved enough to buy the fabric for the dresses. I'm counting on a good profit."

Tierney touched her abdomen. "Oh, the baby likes the dress too." She walked across the big room to the kitchen table. She took her mug and took a sip of coffee and some dribbled down onto the dress.

"Oh no! What you must think of me!"

"Take it off and I can get the stain out."

Tierney frowned and her eyes looked moist. "I burned my other one. It was dreadful."

"I've worn dresses in worse shape than the one you had. Didn't you think to ask me first?"

"I was convinced you'd agree with me."

There was nothing left to say. Laura Lee had a lock she'd used on her bedroom door when the gang lived at the house. She took the rest of the dresses, set them on her bed and then put the lock through a latch on the door. She hadn't even sewn herself a new dress. She still had the altered ones others had given her.

She swallowed her anger. It was too late now. She couldn't bring herself to glance at Tierney as she walked to the kitchen counter. The loaf of bread was gone. The near empty jam jar was left uncovered and now there were flies everywhere.

Wearily she turned around and leaned against the counter. "I think ground rules need to be established. I know I told you to help yourself, but you ate all the bread and you must have had more than an inch of jam on each piece. I don't have a big supply of food here. I spent days making jam of all different kinds and I traded them for four chickens and a rooster. They'll be delivered in two days. Tomorrow I'll mend the chicken coop. It needs a lot of mending. When I returned home this place was a pigsty. It took a lot of hard work to make it livable. Now little by little I'm making the outside presentable." She sighed. "Where did you say you lived with your parents? It couldn't have been a farm."

Tierney smirked. She pulled a gun from the dress pocket aiming it at Laura Lee. Then she pulled a straw-filled bag out from under her clothes.

Fear and confusion washed over Laura Lee.

"I don't understand. You're not pregnant."

Tierney stood. "Of course, you don't. A pigsty? La de da you must have high expectations. No wonder your brother hated you."

"You knew my brother?"

"I was his woman, and this house is mine." She went to the front door and shot once. "There, the others will be here soon. You might as well sit. Don't you have dresses to sew?"

Laura Lee kept her gaze on Tierney as she sat down. "What others?"

"Henry, and the rest. They joined up after you left. Henry brought me here, and I took over your chores. We each rode in different directions when we heard about Ed and the rest. I stayed away during the day but always came back to sleep. Don't tell me you had no idea your brother had smaller bands of people across the territory."

"I hadn't seen my brother in two years. I wanted no part of this life."

"We heard everything about you sneaking off. Your brother and the men needed you. You're nothing but a traitor. We heard from Dodge you were alive. He disguised himself as a Pinkerton. He'd hoped to save your brother but then he tried to get to you. I can only imagine how people bowed and scraped to him as a Pinkerton." Tierney laughed.

There was no running now, but she planned to watch and wait for an opportunity. Unless they planned to kill her, but why bother? She was another pair of hands to help around the place.

The door slammed open, and three unwashed men walked in, their boots hitting the wooden floor with every step.

One of them stopped in front of her. "You must be Laura Lee Bannock. I'm Henry the leader of this group." He spit on the floor. "It's a good thing to have you here. Right Jaime? No more looking for you. Though that was your brother's thing. We could care less about you. I'm not convinced we need you, so you best make yourself useful."

She shivered.

"Did you hear me?" Henry demanded? "You answer when I talk to you."

"Yes, I can make myself useful."

Jaime took a step toward her. "Any of those McKeegans coming for you?"

"No, I had no reason to stay."

Henry pulled Tierney in for a hug. She looked all too willing.

"This is Benny and the small one is Shot," Jaime told her.

Neither acknowledged her.

"I have to say the house looks good, real good," Jaime commented. "I saw the garden when I rode by. No wonder Ed wanted you back."

Tierney pulled away from Henry. "She's a regular wonder. Chickens are being delivered in two days so tomorrow is fixing the chicken coop day. She traded jam for the chickens. She also makes dresses and sells them. She's saving for a cow. I looked but I couldn't find her stash of money."

Benny and Shot sat down but Jaime stared at her. "Why didn't the McKeegans want you?"

"I didn't want them to be burdened by me. They were very kind and treated me like family but there was too much gossip and they deserved better." Her throat burned. She missed Caden every day.

"You won't be a burden here. You'll earn your keep," Jaime told her.

"Yes," she croaked afraid of being slapped if she didn't answer.

He turned and looked at Tierney. "She make that dress?"

"Yes, she did."

"She gave it to you?"

She shook her head and gave him a coy smile. "I took it for myself."

"I don't want you taking things without asking me first. She's saving for a cow."

Tierney crossed her arms in front of her. "You're not in charge!"

"I'm making myself in charge of this gal and the farm." Jaime stared at Tierney until she glanced away.

Jaime pulled a chair in front of Laura Lee and sat. "Now tell me about your plans for the farm."

"I want it to provide for me. Of course, sugar, flour, and coffee would have to be bought but I came here without money. The chickens will provide eggs and more chickens. Eventually I'll have enough they will be a source of food. The cow will provide milk that I can churn into butter and hopefully trade, and my mother used to make cheese. I'll need to find her recipe but that could be another resource. I also plan to put up as much as I can to get me through the winter. The reason Tierney didn't find money is because I don't have any. I bought material, buttons and thread for the dresses."

"I thought you were saving for a cow."

"I am. I figured with my investment into the fabric I could double my money. Right now, I'm not sure how much I'll get. One dress makes a difference. But that was all before you all came."

"We have enough for you to buy new material," Jaime told her.

"What! You never had money for me!" Tierney shrieked.

"Tierney," Henry warned.

She pouted her lips.

"Shot, go skin those rabbits we caught, and the girls can make us some food," Henry told him.

Shot nodded and went out the door but not before Laura Lee caught sight of his long knife.

She was back where she'd started but worse.

Chapter Twenty-One

"Caden come to the house. I know Myles would love to see you," Cait said. She sat on her horse next to Caden's, both admiring the view of Rosemary Valley.

"Your new house sure is something. You and Myles are lucky to have each other. But I'm going to turn you down, Cait. I'm not good company these days."

Cait nodded and gave him a sad smile. "Have you decided if you're going after Laura Lee?"

"At first, I was ready to go off halfcocked, but she knows where I am if she needs me. I'll be fine. I thought things were going in a good direction for us, but she left. Cait, she didn't even say goodbye. That's what rubs the most. I think my ego took a blow is all."

Cait's eyebrows shot upward. "Your ego? Try your heart, Caden. Sometimes you just have to reach for what you want. You need answers, so get them. If you think she's worth it, I mean." She turned her horse and rode off toward the other side of the valley where the new house was.

Caden stared into the distance. *Ma, what advice would you have given me? I miss you.*

The valley certainly was beautiful. He turned Rumble around and rode home. Why couldn't he decide what to do? He wasn't usually so indecisive, was he? No one seemed to know why she left. All her friends had been surprised to discover she was gone. He had waited, thinking she'd be back. He was certain she'd write to him, but all the waiting only led to heartache.

He never felt so alone. He had love inside him that was unwanted, and he didn't know what to do with it or any of his other feelings. He needed to face her, but could he bring himself to do it?

He'd known for a few weeks where she was. It wasn't all that far away. It was just closer to another town. Cait was right, though, he needed answers. It would take a lot of courage to show up at her home. Did he have enough? He couldn't stop thinking of her, dreaming of her. He couldn't stand not knowing.

And... he needed to be sure she was fine.

He swung down from his leather saddle and handed the reins to Phil, one of the older boys who had lived at the orphanage until he'd grown up. He lived in the bunkhouse now.

Caden needed to ask Nessa to make him provisions to take, and he also needed to talk to his pa. He walked through the house and entered his pa's office, seating himself in one of the comfortable chairs in front of the desk.

"Something on your mind, son?"

"Too much, Pa. I'm going after Laura Lee. If she has a husband by now, I need to know. I can't sit here waiting and wondering anymore. The questions gnaw at me."

Eion nodded. "I was wondering if you would go. I figured you would, but as time went on..."

"I can't hide out here on the ranch anymore. I'm swallowing my pride, and I'm going to find out why she left me. Maybe I just imagined she felt the same as me. At the very least I know we were good friends." He met his father's gaze and took a deep breath. "I'm leaving in the morning."

A warm smile spread across his pa's face. "I'm proud of you, son. It takes a lot to swallow one's pride. I don't think it'll take much convincing. You two belong together. She's been through a lot. Maybe she needed to sort through it all. Have a safe journey and remember not to push too hard for answers."

"Thanks, Pa. I'm not sure how long I'll be gone."

"Take as long as is needed."

Caden swallowed hard before he stood and walked out of his father's office.

Laura Lee was right back where she'd been. Her dreams began to die, one by one. At first, she looked for a way to escape, but she was never alone. She toiled while Tierney watched her. Henry didn't seem to think anything of it, but Jaime told the younger girl more than once to start helping. Tierney didn't help, but she claimed credit for meals and clean clothes.

Laura Lee didn't care. Henry looked at Tierney as if she was an angel. Jaime was clearly growing more and more disgusted with the whole thing. Shot and Benny seemed content to watch everything play out.

Every afternoon and long into the evening Laura Lee sewed. Tierney claimed she was best at making deals so she'd been the one to go to town to trade. She'd come back with new fabric, a bit of money, and a present she'd bought herself. If Mr. Beeves mentioned jam, Laura Lee was out picking berries for the next few days. It didn't matter how hot it was, she'd have to stand over steaming pots all day stirring the jam.

The only time she had to think was when she lay before the fire at night. Jaime slept on the sofa guarding her. She prayed and thought about Caden and how much she missed him. Maybe he'd found himself a nice girl. Maybe even the new schoolteacher. It would be for the best, but her heart cracked a bit more when she thought about it.

With the way everyone was eating, they'd be starved by Christmas. Maybe they'd abandon her then. An unlikely thought.

Thundering hoofbeats signaled that a rider was approaching fast. As much as she wanted to run to the window, she stayed in the kitchen cutting up deer meat Jaime had brought back from his morning hunt. At least he dressed it and all. They'd have venison steaks tonight, and then tomorrow she'd spend the day canning the meat.

A rather tall man barged into the house. "Where is Henry?" He looked at both women and his gaze stayed on Tierney. "Where is he?"

"Scouting a new job. That's all I know."

"Where is everyone else?"

"Jaime is out back stretching a deer skin, and Shot went with Henry. There is just Laura Lee and me in here. I have no idea what happened to Benny." Her voice had the slightest quaver to it, but she didn't show fear.

The man looked dangerous in his buckskins and unruly hair. He had a knife and hatchet on his belt as well as his rifle in one hand.

He paused and swept a hard gaze over Laura Lee. "So, you're Laura Lee. You're a pretty thing. Too bad we don't have time to get acquainted. Pack up what you need for a few days. A posse is about a day out."

She put her hand over her heart. "You could leave me here. I could send them in another direction," she offered.

"Now, miss, it's either come or die. I'm the leave-no-witnesses type of man." His eyes bored into her.

"In that case I need to pack a few bags. There's only your horse and Jaime's here. Are we taking the horses or am I walking with a pack on my back?"

Tierney and the tall man stared at her.

"I need to know because carrying too much on my back slows me down." She tilted her chin up.

"Name's Jimbo by the way. You'll do. We'll be doing both. When we get to the mountains the horses will carry the load. Tierney, get a move on!"

Tierney's mouth opened and closed. Then she snapped, "Laura Lee, get to it!"

Chapter Twenty-Two

She'd sworn never to wear trousers again, but now she was grateful she'd kept them. It had been hard going, all uphill or so it seemed. Laura Lee rode double with Jimbo, and for some reason Tierney hadn't liked that arrangement.

Jimbo was bigger and took up more space. Tierney was welcome to him, but he didn't like her. She challenged him a few times telling him he wasn't in charge. That didn't go over so well with Jimbo. Jaime just smirked and shook his head.

Laura Lee had no idea where they were. They travel one way then it seemed as though they would backtrack and go another way covering their tracks. They'd changed direction so often she was confused. She'd never be able to find her way out of the mountains.

If they were lucky, they'd come upon a cave to spend the night in. There were enough creeks and springs to find water, and Jaime was always able to find a squirrel or rabbit to eat. She did all the cooking and cleaning. Tierney was always tired. Jimbo threatened to leave Tierney behind, but she didn't seem to care. She was waiting for her Henry to come and rescue her.

It was confusing. Who was Tierney loyal to? She had gone from Ed to Henry and now Jimbo, but he didn't want her. She'd probably cajoled her way out of doing work with the first two men. The condition she'd found the house in proved that.

They finally stopped for the day. They had walked a lot of it. Laura Lee's legs were too short to keep up with the men, but she tried. At one point they thought they'd lost Tierney and neither man seemed to care. But she popped up an hour later.

"Wish you'd found a cave," Tierney griped now.

"There isn't a cave at every turn, now is there?" Jaime snapped. "Help make the fire."

It was hard to ignore the constant bickering.

"What are you doing with that pot? Just roast the rabbit like usual." Tierney shook her head as though she would even know what she was talking about.

Laura Lee ignored her. "Jimbo, can I borrow your knife?"

Tierney laughed. "You are such a fool. No one with a brain will give you a knife."

"What do you need cutting, I'll do it." Jimbo and Jaime always cut for her.

"I found wild onions and dandelions. I want to chop the meat and onions. Besides why would I kill you before you led me out of the mountains?"

Jaime chuckled.

Jimbo handed her his big knife. "You have a point."

Laura Lee found herself smiling for the first time in days. "I need more water. I—"

"I'll get it!" Tierney grabbed two canteens and stomped off.

"Well, imagine that. Tierney is trying to be useful," Jimbo commented. "How long was she with Henry?"

Jaime lifted one shoulder and then let it fall. "Since the day we found out Ed had been caught. I don't think Henry particularly cares for her."

"We should meet up with Henry in a few days. Then she won't be my problem," Jimbo told him.

"You could just let me go at that point. I really don't know anything." Laura Lee clenched her jaw waiting for an answer.

"I already told you, no witnesses. Besides the men will enjoy having a pretty female around."

She swallowed hard. "What does that mean, Jimbo?" Her voice was whispery.

"It means just the way it sounds. I already have two wives. I see no need for another," Jimbo told her.

Quickly she leaned over, keeping her head down. A tear trailed down her face. Since none of the men had paid her that type of attention, she'd let her guard down and pushed it to the back of her mind.

"Ow!" She dropped the knife and grabbed a cloth. Her finger was bleeding a surprising amount. Breathing raggedly, she backed up and leaned against a boulder. Tears started to fall. She'd tried and tried to be strong, but knowing what her fate was to be was too much.

Jaime held out a hand and helped her to her feet then guided her toward the fire and persuaded her to sit. He sat next to her; his saddle bag was in front of him.

"Let me take a look."

She held out her hand. It shook.

"It's going to be fine," Jaime reassured her. He gently unwrapped her finger and looked, then he grabbed his canteen and poured water over it.

"It's going to need stitches. Jimbo got any rot gut on you?"

"For a finger? I'm not wasting my whiskey on a finger!"

She closed her eyes. Jimbo's true colors were coming to light. She drew in a deep breath and prayed.

"I'll be fine, Jaime. It's not the first time I've had stitches. If I cry don't feel bad."

He studied her for a moment before he threaded the needle. "I'll be quick."

She gave him a fleeting smile and tried to hold still. She kept herself from crying out but there was no help for the tears. Jaime kept his promise and made it relatively quick. He wrapped her finger with a clean cloth.

Before she had a chance to wipe her tears, Tierney appeared with the canteens and an armful of mushrooms.

"Grow up. Did Jimbo make you wife number three? There's no getting out of it. You have to be claimed by one of the men." Tierney set everything down near the pot. "Here you go, and you are welcome."

A wave of cold swept over Laura Lee. Tierney was right, she did need to grow up. She also needed to smarten up. Knowing God was with her gave her courage.

"Thank you, Jaime. I'll finish up making supper." She wiped away her tears, stood and gave him a watery smile.

After cleaning the knife she started putting everything together, searing the meat and then adding the onion. The mushrooms needed to be wiped off. She finished wiping off the first one when she realized the mushrooms were poisonous. She paused.

Could she add them and take her chances getting away? She'd have two horses and supplies to get back to Langford; back to Caden. Temptation was everywhere and she needed to be strong enough to keep from falling into it. Swiping up the mushrooms, she headed away from camp.

"Hey where are you going with the mushrooms? You hate that I'm adding to the meal, don't you?"

Laura Lee had hoped to talk to Tierney privately after she disposed of the mushrooms. There was bound to be trouble.

"It's better to be rid of them," she explained lamely.

"Bring them here," Jimbo told her.

Slowly she walked over to where Jimbo sat. "They're poisonous. It's hard to tell the difference."

"Get rid of them."

She stepped over brush, rocks and fallen branches. She wanted to be far enough away the horses wouldn't find them. She dropped them under a bush and headed back. Did she just throw away her only chance at freedom? It didn't matter, she couldn't kill them. Killing was a huge sin. She'd already racked up enough sins for a lifetime.

"Jaime you didn't need to come after me." Of course, he'd trailed her.

"I wanted to talk to you for a moment, alone." His voice was gentle but she tensed up anyway.

"I know you're a good woman. You remind me of my mother in that she had a good heart too. My pa died and a new man married her. I watched her become more and more unhappy. The light in her eyes faded. She never smiled anymore. Then one day she just didn't wake up. I can't allow that to happen to you. But I can't let you walk away either. Jimbo would shoot you." He sighed then drew another deep breath. "I've given it some thought, and I will claim you."

She tried to get around him. Claiming was the last thing she wanted.

Gentle hands cupped her shoulders. "Hey, don't worry. You've never..."

Her face heated, and she could imagine just how fiery red she was. "I—I'm saving myself for marriage."

"Don't worry. I wouldn't... But people must think we are. You need to stay near me and act like you love me."

"How do I do that?"

"I'll kiss you now and then, and hand holding is good. A hug occasionally would look good. And smile at me. One rule, never push me away. If I'm to save your virtue, the others must believe you're mine. Can you do that?"

"You are a good man, Jaime. Thank you, and I will take you up on your offer."

Now you need to look the part. He let her hair down and mussed it.

"Bite your lips so you look well kissed, and pretend you hate me. But... only hate me for an hour or two."

"You're going to a lot of trouble for me." She hated the idea but if it kept her safe it would be worth it. Would he keep his word?

"I happen to think you're worth it." His eyes softened.

Chapter Twenty-Three

It had been so long since he'd bathed, he swore his clothes could stand up on their own. He'd been about one day out from Laura Lee's place when he found himself on the wrong end of a gun. He hadn't even made a fire that night but he was found and captured.

Caden made sure to be useful enough. They were beginning to trust him. Things had been uneasy at first. He'd thought for sure someone would recognize him. But there hadn't been a flicker of recognition.

They were currently on the run from a posse. Caden hoped he didn't end up dangling from the end of a rope, found guilty through association. He'd learned much by listening. These men would lead him to Laura Lee, he was certain. They each had an outlandish story of how Ed Bannock practically walked barefoot across hot coals. In their eyes, he was some sort of saint.

It was crazy how much they'd looked up to Ed. But Henry was in charge now. He was smart enough to keep them from being caught.

There had been a trap waiting for them at the Bannock property. Henry'd had a feeling in his bones. He sent one of the others to creep up and find out, and sure enough men were hiding in the woods around the property.

It had been a relief to learn the house was empty, but it was also a huge concern. Where was Laura Lee? If what Caden had heard was true, she was traveling with a woman and part of the deadly gang. They revered her for being Ed's sister. That had been a relief to find out. Maybe she was safe... for the time being.

"We're getting closer," Caden told Henry. "They were here not more than a day ago."

"Glad you're such a good tracker, Smith. You've come in handy a time or two."

Caden didn't want praise. He was hopeful when he saw two sets of women's tracks. Laura Lee was still alive. They might possibly be able to catch up to them tomorrow. Then his real worries would start. How would he get her out of there?

"Mount up, daylight is burning. Smith, I want you out front. It's hard going in these mountains so have a care where your horse steps."

Caden led his horse out front. He swung into the saddle and carefully navigated through the rocky pass through the mountains. They kept going well after dark, all leading their horses instead of riding.

"Boss, they're about a quarter of a mile out. I see their fire," Caden told Henry.

"Idiots, they should know better than have a fire out in the open. Let's keep going. We'll stop when we're closer so I can call out. I'd hate to have come all this way just to get shot."

It didn't take long before they yelled to the camp and walked in. It had been a long day. Caden scanned the area for Laura Lee and when he saw her bedroll right next to one of the men's, anger besieged him. He wanted to grab her up and take her home, but they'd have to play it all out until they could safely leave.

Jimbo had been ribbing them all since they came back to camp. The tousled hair worked. The fact that she couldn't stop blushing probably didn't hurt any. Jaime and Jimbo exchanged a knowing grin. How had she gotten herself into this position?

"I thought you'd gotten lost," Tierney spouted.

"No, just burying the deadly mushrooms is all."

"*You* say they're deadly, but I know the difference. You just want to look like some type of hero. Well, it worked. You got yourself claimed, though I thought Jaime had better standards."

"Tierney," Jaimie warned.

"You might as well get supper done, Laura Lee. Jimbo is hungry."

She finished making the soupy stew. It wasn't half bad. Jaime and Jimbo complemented her while Tierney glared at her. She was just as glad to get away from the other woman when she cleaned up.

When she was done, she walked to the fire. Her bedroll was next to Jaime's. He'd told her it would be that way, yet it stunned her. Tierney was busy kissing Jimbo. Probably so he forgot she almost poisoned them.

"Hello, the camp!"

Jaime pulled his gun and pushed her down onto the bedroll.

"It's Henry," Jimbo told them. He attempted to push Tierney away but it was too late. Henry had his gun drawn and his expression was deadly as he stared at the couple.

"This is how it's been? Tierney answer me," Henry demanded.

Terror flared in Tierney's eyes. "I didn't think you were coming back. When we had to leave the house, I thought it wise to get a new protector."

"You'd best decide right now, me or Jimbo. We all have to do what we must to stay safe, but I'm back."

Jimbo looked as though he wanted to shove Tierney off his lap.

She stood quickly. "It's you I love."

He gave her a curt nod.

"This must be Laura Lee. Jaime, you are one lucky son of a gun. You're family, Laura Lee, we're glad to have you with us. We picked up a man during our travels. This is Smith." He gestured toward Caden. We also lost Johnson Levitt. Took a bullet for me. He might have been a lousy Pinkerton but he was one of the best we had.

Laura Lee barely kept from gasping when her gaze met Caden's hard cold stare. He didn't look at all happy to see her. Why was he here?

"Smith," Jaime greeted with a nod. "Where do you hail from?"

"Down near Texas." He showed no emotion. "Had to kill my wife, and I thought it best to ride north."

As much as she needed to soak in the sight of him, she was compelled to glance away, while shame filled her. What must he think of her? She needed to talk to him, but it wasn't going to be tonight.

"I could heat up some beans for you," she offered.

"No, you stay with Jaime. I don't think I've ever seen him smile before. Tierney can feed us," Henry said.

Tierney didn't say a word. Instead, she hurried to make Henry happy.

"Ed's absent sister. He was obsessed with finding you. It was probably his downfall. No woman is worth getting killed over. You're right pretty, though." Henry's smile chilled her.

She didn't know where to look. She stared down at her hands which were soon covered by Jaime's hands. A deep breath filled her, steadied her and she glanced up and smiled at Jaime. No matter what she had to play along, or they'd end up dead.

Chapter Twenty-Four

U pon first spotting Laura Lee in the camp, it was as though a big weight was lifted off Caden's shoulders. It didn't take long, though, to feel more weight being added, much more.

He sat around the fire accepting coffee from the other female. Tierney? Yes, that was her name. She wasn't the most cordial woman. Caden tried everything to not glance at Laura Lee. It galled him how close she sat next to that giant of a man.

The giant was currently washing and rebandaging Laura Lee's finger. It wasn't that he didn't want to look his fill, but it was too dangerous. Just how close was Laura Lee with the other man? People did what they had to when they were trying to survive, but he didn't have to like it.

"Jaime, how long have you and Ed's sister been together?" Henry asked.

"As of this afternoon." Jaime subjected Henry to a hard stare. "She's a gem, and I didn't want to wait and let any of you horn in. She has been claimed and I don't expect any trouble out of any of you."

Laura Lee stared at her hands again.

The giant was Jaime. Now what was involved in "claiming a woman"? Caden's stomach churned as he thought of the possibilities. Thankfully Jaime acted gentle toward her. Not that Caden was in any position to stand up for her. Hopefully that would change.

"Where'd you find such a treasure?" Caden asked. If Jaime's glare was any indication, he shouldn't have asked.

"She was living in the Bannock house. She made amazing changes for the better. It was filthy before with trash everywhere. When I got there, the floors had even been scrubbed. The garden looked as if it would actually yield something. She made jam and dresses to barter. She was saving for a cow." Jaime's voice was full of pride.

"Where's the money now?" Henry asked.

Laura Lee looked at Henry. "I invested the money in material and whatever else I needed to sew. I was making a nice little profit before Tierney decided to help herself to one of the dresses and buy herself things. That pushed back the purchase of a cow by over a month."

"Quite the little businesswoman, aren't you?" Henry looked at her with appreciation. "One dress made such a difference?"

"When you are counting pennies, it is. I already had chickens delivered. I was able to can some of the meat Jaime brought back from his hunting excursions. I figured if I was careful, I'd make it through the winter. Jaime was going to show me how to soften a deer pelt."

"Almost like married folk," Jimbo joked.

"I'm impressed. I didn't think anything could be done with the place." Henry stared at Tierney.

"Nothing a little soap, water, and determination couldn't handle," murmured Laura Lee.

Tierney pulled a knife from her pocket. She swiftly got to her feet and started around the fire toward Laura Lee. Caden jumped to his feet, but he was too far away. Thankfully, Jaime disarmed her.

"You go too far!" Jaime roared.

Henry was on his feet. He carried Tierney off behind some boulders. She could be heard crying.

Laura Lee couldn't believe what had almost happened. Tierney's attitude toward working had been bothering everyone. Even if that woman was jealous, she had no cause to pull a knife. Why wasn't she just happy to have Henry back? Though Henry wasn't a prize.

Henry returned. Tierney appeared with a pot full of beans to heat over the fire. Laura Lee started to get up, but Henry shook his head at her.

She risked a glance at Caden and again wondered what he must think about her. No matter what she did, her reputation turned to mud. Before she'd run away from home, she'd never gotten into situations like this. She caught Caden's gaze for a brief moment but the disgust she saw broke her.

He wasn't here to help her. He wasn't part of the gang either. Maybe the sheriff sent him as a spy? It was so hard to know. It didn't matter, humiliation still filled her. Going to bed was going to be so hard. Her bedroll was so close to Jaime's.

It might be easier to walk away and get lost for bit. This was not going to end well.

"You're shaking," Jaime whispered as he looked into her eyes. He put his arm around her shoulder, pulling her closer. For the moment she felt safe and protected. The best thing she could do for Caden was to forget him.

That night she barely slept.

Lord, please don't let me give Caden away. I don't want to get him killed. I can handle anything but him dying. I'm doing everything I can to be virtuous. Maybe You could get the posse to go home? Thank You for sending Jaime to protect me. I don't know how he ended up as part of the Bannock Gang. There is much good inside him.

The next morning there was much grumbling about continuing without breakfast. There was supposedly a secret house not too far away. Everyone walked. The trail was tight and full of fallen rocks.

A few of the men, including Caden, went ahead to clear the path as much as possible. At one point the path was rock on one side and a sheer drop off on the other side. Jaime reached for her hand and helped her. Behind her she heard Henry threaten to throw Tierney down the mountain side. He sounded like he meant it.

Jaime gave her hand a quick squeeze. "Don't look down. Concentrate on me. Maybe you could think about how handsome I am." She laughed and the high tension she'd felt was gone.

Once they got through that dangerous part there sat a house. Who would have built a house way out here? The log cabin looked spacious and in good condition.

"Who lives here?" she asked.

"It belonged to Jimbo's family. His wives live here now. They are both very nice. He calls them his rescues. He found them wandering the mountains."

"At the same time?" she asked.

"No, Reina was found first and then Marta. Jimbo lived here alone, and he claimed them both," Jaime explained.

"I'm in no position to judge but I like the one wife way of life better."

Jaime laughed and kissed the top of her head.

They watched as two young women ran out the house straight to Jimbo. The hugs and kisses were proof of their happiness.

"I need to talk to you alone sometime today."

She bit her bottom lip. What could he want to talk to her about?

"It's nothing bad. I just think we need a plan is all."

Smiling, she nodded to him. "I'll find the time."

Chapter Twenty-Five

Reina and Marta filled the massive dining table with food. Laura Lee offered to help but the two women told her to have a seat. She looked much better cleaned up and wearing a fresh dress. He didn't see a bruise on her and breathed easier.

Caden tried to be inconspicuous when he glanced at Laura Lee. She didn't smile at Jaime the same way she'd smiled at him. A plan for escape was foremost in his mind. If the posse showed up it would be shoot first and ask questions later. His concern for Laura Lee's safety grew.

There was such a difference between the way Jaime treated Laura Lee and the way Henry treated Tierney. Had Ed treated Tierney the same way? It was sad to see. He didn't open his mouth. There'd be no suspicion thrown his way.

Jimbo and his wives looked happy. It was an unusual arrangement and while he couldn't condemn it, he couldn't approve either. It wasn't his business.

He almost laughed at the way the men suddenly had manners. They hadn't exhibited any the whole time he'd been with them.

Now that he'd been shown their hideout, they'd never willingly allow him to leave. He needed time to see if there was a different way off this mountain. He glanced at Laura Lee and found himself glared at by Jaime. The key was to be extra careful. It was hard not to watch her, though.

She was certainly a woman to admire. She handled herself very well. All of the things she'd done at her home sounded amazing, but she'd always been determined. He should have gone to get her much

sooner. None of this would be happening now if he had.

It was hard to be with the others in the gang. They were loud, and all they talked about was women and booze. He laughed at their jokes, but he had nothing to add.

Laura Lee finally persuaded Marta and Reina to allow her to help in the kitchen. She was busy cutting biscuits when Jaime appeared.

"Ready?" he asked.

She quickly wiped her hands on a towel. "I'm ready." Her back was hurting from the tension. What had she done wrong? Had there been an objection to the claiming? If only she knew the rules.

Holding hands, they walked through the woods until they came upon a view that was awe inspiring. There was a river way down below. Wildflowers grew close to the banks.

Jaime lifted her and set her upon a high flat rock before joining her.

She wrung her hands waiting for him to begin the talk.

"You're too good for this place, Laura Lee. I'd like to find a way to get you away from these men. They aren't honorable like me and Jimbo. You are sweet, kind, and decent. I'd hate for you to lose those qualities, and if I wait too long, I won't be able to let you go. I'm starting to grow attached to you."

"Should I fear for my safety if you're not around?"

"I think your friend Smith can handle things, but I wouldn't be surprised if he got shot for his trouble."

Stunned she stared at Jaime. "How do you know about Smith?"

"I've been tuned into your moods, and I can see how you two look at one another. When you aren't trying to ignore one another that is. He'll end up dead if we don't get him out of here quickly. He's not drinking enough rotgut and the men are getting suspicious. Will he be good to you?"

Her face heated. "I know he will. While I was on the run I ended up disguised as a nun. The town was so kind, and I had a nice life. But Ed came to town, and I ran again. Caden, I mean Smith came after me. I taught at the orphanage and people in town liked me. When I came back there were too many whispers and it wasn't fair to Caden or his family. I thought it better I leave."

"Sorry you left?"

"Yes and no. No because I had fixed up the house and was making enough money to survive the winter. It was a great feeling of accomplishment. At the same time, I was lonely.

Not because I was alone, it was because I thought I'd never see Caden again."

"You love him," Jaime stated.

She hesitated and then nodded. "Yes, I'd never been in love before. Leaving made a big hole in my heart."

"He feels the same way?" Jaime cocked his head to the side watching her.

"I thought so, but he never once tried to contact me. I know he cares, and we are good friends."

"You know you can't go back to your house, don't you? It might have been burned down. Some posses are ruthless."

She furrowed her brow. "How'd you get involved in all this?"

He shrugged. "I'm wanted by the law. A man shot my pa, and I shot him back. Both ended up dead. There was a whole bar full of people who could swear it was self-defense. The sheriff was escorting me to the jail when Henry came through shooting. He had an extra horse and told me to get on. I've never had to kill anyone else, and for that I'm thankful. The moment I saw you I knew you shouldn't be around us."

She put her hand on his. "You did me the greatest favor by claiming me. You're right though, I've been on the wrong end of some evil stares. I'm not sure they can all be trusted. You deserve better."

"I'm lucky I'm not locked up. We leave tomorrow at first light. We're going hunting and we need Smith to claim to be the best hunter. I'll lead you down a rarely used path. I'll come back hours later saying you got the jump on me. Smith..." He smiled. "...Caden can take it from there. I'll need two things. I need you to kiss me like you love me in front of the men. Then

I'll accuse Caden of looking at you the wrong way and haul him off for a talk. I need to let him know not to try to shoot me."

Kiss him in front of the men? Her heart fluttered. "I can do it."

"Trust me. That's all I ask," he said leaning over to kiss her forehead. He lifted her off the rock and held her hand back to the house.

There were good men in the world. Hopefully, Jaime would find his way out of his troubles and come to lead a normal life. He deserved a wife and family. It was going to be hard to say goodbye.

Chapter Twenty-Six

Caden narrowed his eyes when he watched Laura Lee and Jaime walk through the door. They'd been gone long enough. Too long. This situation was tricky at best. Would Laura Lee leave with him? She'd known this life before, and now with Jaime...

He wasn't leaving without telling her how he felt about her. She'd have to look at him and tell him she wanted to stay. How to get her alone, hmm.

"Yo, Smith! I need a word with you," Jaime said in a hard voice.

"I don't have much I want to hear," Caden replied. Where was this leading?

"You can come with me, or I'll drag you away. Your choice." Jaime's stare was daunting.

Caden slowly stood. No need to let Jaime think his threats had worked. He made sure not to glance at Laura Lee as he followed the big man outside.

Jaime walked a long distance from the house and stopped suddenly.

"What's this about?" Caden asked, annoyed.

"It's Laura Lee. I want you to get her out of here. She's too good for this life. I'd hate to see the light in her eyes slowly die."

"You expect me to sneak her off the mountain? I don't have a death wish. You planning on following at a later date?"

"Listen Caden, I know who you are and more importantly I know what you are to Laura Lee. There's nothing between us except for respect and friendship. I pretended to claim her to keep her safe. To tell you the truth, though, I'm not sure how long my claim will keep the other men away."

Caden nodded, but his heart thundered at this new turn. "How am I supposed to get her out of here?"

"Tomorrow at first light I'm going to tell everyone I'm going hunting. I want you to volunteer to come with me. Say you've hunted plenty, call yourself a great hunter. Then I'll insist Laura Lee come with me. We'll leave false trails. Then I'll show you a secret path. You'll have to hit me with your gun. It'll have to be hard enough to make my head bleed. I'll wander back to the house around dusk. They'll want to go after you, but It'll be too late."

"You'd do all that for us?"

Jaime chuckled. "Not for you. I'm doing this for Laura Lee. I'm relying on you to take good care of her. Like I said, I see the way she looks at you. It's not easy giving up the only woman I've cared about, but it's for her happiness I'm doing this. Are you in or do I have to shoot you?"

"It's a good plan. I'm impressed. You won't need to worry about her. She doesn't know it yet, but I plan to marry her."

Jaime clenched his jaw then gave a weak smile and nodded. "I figured as much. I'll handle all objections tomorrow. A few won't like you going, and there will be some who want me to leave Laura Lee behind. You just get ready to leave. I'll see what supplies I can get my hands on."

"I appreciate it."

"Now go back and look mad. I told you to stop watching my woman. I'll stay here for a few more minutes."

Caden nodded and started for the house. It was better than any plan he'd come up with. They wouldn't have horses. Leaving Rumble behind was going to be hard.

It was unnerving, waiting for the two men to come back. Everyone was watching the door waiting for them to return.

Caden came in and made it obvious he wasn't going to glance in her direction.

"I'm surprised your face isn't bleeding," Jimbo commented.

"I expected a black eye," Henry added. "What did Jaime want?"

"It was a friendly conversation about not looking at his woman. The next conversation will probably result in me being maimed."

Everyone but Laura Lee laughed.

Jaime came through the door. He met her gaze and smiled. He was by her side, lifting her and then setting her on his lap, before she knew what was happening.

She laid her head against his shoulder. He held her tighter than ever, and she understood how much he truly cared for her. He'd been a blessing. Tomorrow was going to be a tense one. Would she make it out of here with Caden? She'd pray on it.

All night long she tossed and turned. Sleep was impossible. She'd gone over everything that could happen and it scared her.

"You'll need your sleep," Jaime told her.

"I'm sorry it must be hard enough to sleep on the floor and now I've woken you up with my restlessness."

"I've been dozing on and off. I'm hoping all goes well."

There was silence for a few minutes.

"I'll miss you, Laura Lee. You are a special lady. I'm thinking about changing my name and heading out to California. I want a life like you and Caden will have."

"I hope that happens for you, Jaime. I'll miss you. I hope you don't get in trouble when they discover we're gone."

"It's a chance I'm willing to take. Now, get some sleep."

She turned over and slept.

Chapter Twenty-Seven

There was a tense moment at the breakfast table when Caden volunteered to go hunting with Jaime. Jaime sounded a bit reluctant but made plans for them to leave after they ate.

"You're coming too," Jaime told Laura Lee.

"You don't bring women hunting," Jimbo advised.

"This one you do. She spots the animals, and I shoot. Works well. Plus, you don't think I'd leave her behind with the likes of you, do you?" Jaime smiled.

Henry laughed. "Take her so I won't have to smack a few of the men when they get fresh with her."

She started to shake, and Jaime put his arm around her. "We'd best get going. Smith, you have a gun? A rifle would be better."

"I had both before I met up with my new friends here."

"Give Smith his stuff back, will ya?" Jaime grumbled.

Henry got up from the table and went down the hall to his room. He came back out with both the gun and rifle. "I'll even throw in your holster."

"Thanks," Caden said. He grabbed his holster, firearms, and coat. "I'll wait for you outside." He closed the door quietly behind him.

"Keep your eye on Smith. He's been trustworthy so far but now that he has his gun, you never know," Henry warned.

"I'm hoping he's as good at hunting as he says and I won't have to go out all the time," Jaime commented as he stood.

He offered his hand to her, and she stood next to him.

"Why the long face, Laura Lee?" Tierney asked. "Did you think you and Jaime would be alone?" She smirked.

"I didn't sleep so well last night is all."

Everyone chuckled while a few of the men elbowed each other. Let them laugh. She'd be outside soon enough enjoying the fresh air. Bunch of juveniles. Ed was like that after he'd formed the gang.

For once her blushing paid off. She and Jaime gathered a few things and walked out the front door.

"Walk nice and slow," Jaime told them. "Laura Lee, hold my hand. I'm sure they're watching out the window." He squeezed her hand. "You did real good in there, real good."

They walked to the tree line. "This is the way I'd usually go. We'll lay some tracks and then walk round to the other side."

They walked for half an hour before Jaime pointed out a log for Caden to walk on.

"Just stay at the other end of the log. Walk on one and I'll have Laura Lee do the same. I'll wipe away some of my tracks and come back to get you." Still holding her hand, Jaime continued down the trail.

"Why have Caden and I make different trails?" she asked.

"We'd normally split up for a time while hunting. We'd have kept each other in sight so as not to shoot or get shot."

"I'm glad of your knowledge," she said. This time she gave his hand a slight squeeze.

Sure, enough there was another fallen tree and she scurried across it and waited.

Jaime came up from below her. "That should confuse them enough to keep them busy but not so much they'll be suspicious."

They walked until they located Caden. Then they continued, this time heading downward.

Jaime stopped and let her hand go. "There's enough supplies to get you to a safe place. There are several creeks around the mountains. Be sure to keep your canteens full. See that trail there? It's a game trail animals use, mostly deer. Keep to that." He looked at her with sad eyes. "Give me a hug."

She stepped into his arms and hugged him hard. "Thank you for everything."

"Stay here. I'll have Caden walk me back up the trail and then hit me on the head. I'm going to miss you. Good luck."

Her throat burned as her eyes watered. There was so much to say but she couldn't get a word out. It hurt her heart to watch them leave.

Lord please watch over Jaime. He's really such a good man.

She thought about adding a prayer for herself, but she already knew God was with her.

Caden felt uneasy leaving Jaime bleeding, but it was for the best. Plus, Jaime insisted. Caden hurried back down the trail and back to Laura Lee. It was his turn to take her hand. It had been hard to hold his tongue, but he'd done it.

He walked to her held out his hand and when she took it, he was filled with joy. Everything went according to plan. "We'll need to walk a bit faster I think."

She nodded.

"Thinking about Jaime?"

"Yes, I just hope he'll be fine. He took a big gamble helping us."

"He sure did," he agreed. "Let's get off this mountain."

They fought mosquitoes and flies at every turn, but they endured. It was almost dusk when he finally saw the cave Jaime had described. They'd sleep there for one night. Then the plan was to skirt the town of Butte. There were more outlaws than citizens in that place. From there, he knew his way. As long as they stayed off the main roads they'd be just fine.

Luckily, they didn't see another soul during their escape.

A strange quietness grew between Caden and Laura Lee. There was so much he wanted to ask but he continued to wonder if the timing was right. Did he measure up to the men she'd admired such as Gideon and Jaime?

Chapter Twenty-Eight

C aden had been every bit the gentleman the whole trip. That was a problem. He didn't watch her or hold her hand any longer. There was no laughter. Was he sorry he had come after her? It had put him in an awful position. They talked about the weather, the terrain, and how far from the McKeegan ranch they were.

It was a disappointment. She'd held onto such high hopes of them growing closer. If anything, he seemed to maintain his distance. She didn't want him to think she was chasing him, so she followed his lead. The worst part was missing his friendship.

They'd walked through so many beautiful places and saw interesting animals, but she didn't point them out to him.

It was one of those days where nothing seemed to go right. She had slept on a sharp rock and her back hurt. She'd burned the beans and getting the pot clean had been a bear of a task. She'd slipped twice, and now it seemed every branch wanted to snag her hair. She didn't have a hat.

Now Caden was softly whistling as though he didn't have a worry. She was cross and no matter how many times she told herself to shake it off, that didn't happen. Every little thing upset her. Caden walked much faster than she did with his long legs, and she couldn't see him ahead.

Another branch snagged her and this one had her hair in its grip. She couldn't yank it. How could it have gotten so tangled. Why didn't she have a knife? She pulled and pulled until tears ran down her face. She was hopeless, no wonder Caden hardly talked to her.

It stung her heart and refused to go away. The hurt had grown the last couple of days. It made her feel ungrateful and unwanted. Every time Jaime had held her she pictured herself with Caden. What a fool she'd been. She couldn't even think about a future. She had nothing.

She'd worked so hard at her house and things were coming together before Henry showed up. Actually before Tierney came and upset her carefully planned budget. Finding out Tierney wasn't pregnant was the last straw. There was no way she could go back. Everything she'd had was lost to her, including Caden.

With one final hard tug she freed her hair and promptly tripped over her skirt. That was it. She was going to put her pants on. She should have from day one, but she wanted to act a bit ladylike for Caden. Obviously, there had been no reason to try.

Stepping off the path, she changed behind a big tree. With the bandana she found at the bottom of her pack she covered her hair. Hopefully that will help with the snags.

"Where have you been?" Caden demanded, sounding exasperated.

"Changing my clothes. I'm ready let's go."

He studied her and grimaced. "You're going to wear those trousers again?"

She sighed. "Listen, Caden, it's none of your business. Let's just get to somewhere safe."

"None of my business? Really? You've become my business somehow. I don't have to like it, but I feel responsible for you."

Her heart dropped. "I'm sorry to be such a burden," she said quietly. Her mood turned somber. She hurried down the trail, not wanting him to see her tears. She wouldn't want to burden him with her unhappiness.

"Wait up!"

She kept walking. He'd catch up, bypass her, and then leave her far behind. She didn't have to wait. Did he think she'd had inappropriate relations with Jaime? She was done. Why speculate on his reason? He thought her a burden and that was that.

If that was that, why did her heart feel shattered?

"Why didn't you wait?" he demanded.

"You caught up just fine. You walk much faster than me, and I knew you'd be next to me in no time."

"You're in no hurry to get home?"

"Caden, don't try to pick a fight with me, please. I have no home. I have no money or anything that really belongs to me. Even my Bible is gone. If not for God, I'd be alone. These last few years have been a trial, and I just want peace." She slowed her pace, so he'd be ahead of her. She was done talking.

Chapter Twenty-Nine

Laura Lee hadn't had much to say in the last few days. He didn't know how to fix things. She answered with emotionless one-word answers.

Fortunately, they were only a day away from the ranch. Maybe a day or two apart would help things. He wasn't any good at being in love. Everything he said or did was wrong.

A shrill scream came from behind him. Laura Lee! Caden turned back and ran as fast as he could toward her. Laura Lee was already taking her shoe off.

"Snake," she said sounding terrified.

He quickly kneeled at her side and helped her roll up the pant leg and take off her stocking. "What did it look like?"

"Black or brown I don't know. I don't want to die." Tears filled her eyes.

"This is going to hurt." He took his knife and carved and x over the bite. He let it bleed for a bit before he tried to suck out the venom. Let's get you somewhere comfortable where I can build a fire." He took their packs off and put them on the ground. He lifted her and placed her in a clearing leaning against a tree.

"Did you look to make sure there aren't snakes here?"

"I looked. I need to go get our packs." He didn't wait for an answer, just walked over and grabbed the packs. Reaching inside his, he retrieved a canteen and washed out his mouth. Once that was done, he ran back to Laura Lee.

He poured water on the wound and gently soaked up the blood. Next, he set her on a bedroll making certain she continued to sit up. He placed another blanket on top of her. She could die. And that terrified him.

"I want to lie down."

"No, you need your heart higher than the bite. I'm going to make a fire. You'll probably start feeling bad soon."

"Give me a bullet." She held her hand out.

"You want me to shoot you?"

"Of course not. Put the gunpowder on the wound."

"I've never heard of doing that," he told her.

"Give me the bullet and make the fire. I'll need hot water too unless you have whiskey on you." He shook his head.

He got out a bullet and opened it then handed it to her and watched as she first poured it and then pressed a small amount of the powder into the wound.

"Does that absorb the poison?" he asked.

"No. If I start to feel bad, I'll light it. I didn't see the snake and I didn't hear it. Now that I'm calmer, I think it might not have been a rattler."

"That doesn't sound right to me."

"What would you do then?" She stared at him.

"Wait for the fever, give you lots of water and hope for the best."

She shook her head. "The best hope would be to cut off my foot. Let's do it my way. Then I'll just be burned badly but I can keep my limbs intact."

———

Was she already out of her mind? He drew a few deep breaths as he considered her words. Either way they needed the fire. But lighting the gunpowder didn't seem like a very good idea.

He gathered twigs first then small branches. Once he got the fire started, he looked for bigger pieces of wood. He handed Laura Lee the canteen and encouraged her to drink more. He looked at the wound with the gunpowder in it. Where had she gotten such a notion? She was right, though, about people losing limbs after being bit.

"Have you been bit by a snake before?" he asked.

"Not me. Ed was bitten, though," she replied.

"Where was he bit."

"Higher up on his leg." Her eyes widened. "You think I'm crazy don't you? Lighting the gunpowder will not be fun."

"You seem fine. Maybe I got all the venom out."

"I actually think you're right. Either you got it all or the snake wasn't venomous, but I'd like to wait a couple hours to be sure. Just trust me."

He didn't have a choice. He made coffee while they waited.

"You're starting to make me crazy. Trust me," she said.

Trust? He sat and drank his coffee. That's what was missing between them, trust. He loved her but didn't particularly want her to know. He'd trusted her when she had told him Gideon was nothing but a friend. But now? She'd smiled at Jaime too much. They had slept in the same room. She hadn't seemed to want to leave him.

"Whatever is on your mind, you might as well tell me. I didn't get bit on purpose. Just like I didn't get caught by Ed's gang willingly." She softened her tone some. "When I saw you with the men, I was terrified for you. I thought maybe you'd come to see me, and that thrilled me. I'd missed you more than I thought I could miss anyone. I'll always be grateful to Jaime for the help he gave me. He saved me from being treated horribly. It's obvious you don't know me at all." She turned her head.

"I did ride to your place to see you. I missed you too. You didn't even tell me you were leaving. You didn't say goodbye."

"I know. I didn't want you to talk me out of going. I saw the way some of the people in town looked at me, and I didn't want to tarnish your good name. Plus, I didn't think I could walk away from you. You deserve better." She gazed into the fire.

"I think of you as a hero. You escaped your brother and did what you had to."

She shook her head. "People will wonder why I didn't just turn my brother in. A person's name means everything. People trust you to keep your word. They don't question you. I didn't want to muddy your name. I've loved you for a while now. I love you enough to walk away and allow you to live a good life."

He gently touched her cheek, turning her head until she met his gaze. "You thought you were saving me. I'm an idiot. I know you love me."

"Yet you still don't trust me," she added.

"I feel foolish. I do know you. I was jealous because you spent so much time with Jaime. I wish we could have talked about it. Instead, I created a reason not to trust you and that was unfair."

She shifted and winced. "Let's light my foot."

"Are you crazy?"

She laughed. "I must be. I'm sitting here with you, aren't I?"

"I'll warm some water and wash the gunpowder off. No going close to a fire for a while." He leaned over and kissed her. "I love you."

"I love you too."

Chapter Thirty

Things progressed rapidly as soon as they entered the McKeegan house. Pastor Mellon was called right away, and before she realized it, she was married. Not that she didn't choose to wed Caden. It was the fact she craved to at least have a wedding dress. Between Nessa and Mary Jane, Laura Lee hadn't gotten a word in.

Her new sisters-in-law smiled as though everything was so romantic, while her brothers-in-law grinned at Caden. It was hard to trust grins after spending considerable time with men.

She would be protected now because Caden loved her.

"Caden, take a walk with me?" she inquired.

He nodded and offered her his arm. She clung to it tight as they stepped outside.

"What's on your mind?"

She let go of him and took a step back. "Nothing and everything. It's well I'd anticipated my wedding day since I was a girl. I never pictured waiting for your family to be rounded up while I wasn't aware of the reason. It wasn't until Pastor Melon arrived it dawned on me. You never asked me to marry you. I'm still wearing this dress I've had on for a few days and I can only imagine the state of my hair." She sighed as a tear trailed down her face. "I could have changed my clothes and washed up if I knew. Even Nessa and Mary Jane knew, and by the time I found out, it was too late for me to have any input. Now they're planning a coffee and cake reception after church on Sunday?"

She turned from him. "I considered it easier to just proceed with everything, but no one asked what I preferred and when I make a suggestion, I'm ignored. Your father led me to you and the pastor after I almost raced out the door. I heard no one ask you about the wedding. Perhaps it's because I'm used to making my own decisions. I expected we'd make plans together. Instead, I feel as though they herded me to wed you."

"They didn't mean it that way. They all realize how much I love you."

She turned and stepped closer to Caden. "But what about how I feel? They can have their own party on Sunday. I'm not going. Now if you would be so kind as to arrange a bath for me, I'd like to sit here alone and think."

***

Caden nodded and walked inside. The room turned silent as everyone turned and stared.

"Everything okay?" his Pa inquired.

"No. Why didn't one of you at least suggest we change clothes? You all knew. I can't understand with all the women in this house. Not one thought Laura Lee might wish to wash up." He strode further into the room.

"I hadn't proposed to her yet. There is no reason at all we had to have this hasty wedding. Yes, we were alone, but she would never... I need to understand why she has no say in the reception being organized. You can cancel the party. She doesn't wish to go." His heart ached for his wife.

"She's not being difficult; she's just a woman who yearned for a traditional wedding. That means she needed to be asked to wed me. You don't know what it was like out there. All of her choices had been taken away. She was brave and smart and able to escape unscathed. I should have said something, but it didn't occur to me. You are now her only family, but you haven't acted like it. She wants a bath. I'm going to heat some water."

Nessa hustled into the kitchen in front of him. "Aiden, put the bath in their room," she called over her shoulder.

How was she supposed to go back in there? She'd made a fool of herself. She should have counted her blessings instead of counting all the things she'd expected. She would have accepted Caden's proposal and willingly married him.

The last months had been harsh. Even living alone had been rough, but continuing in fear for so long changed her. Maybe she was broken. Ed would be happy.

Could she move back to the orphanage? The surviving members of the Bannock gang didn't know where she'd hidden out. She doubted they'd show their faces in Langford.

Tears blinded her. She cherished Caden, heart and soul. Every part of her being sought to be with him. She wanted to build a life with him. She tensed when she heard someone approaching.

"Oh, my dear. We all got it wrong," Eion acknowledged as he sat next to her on a bench.

She turned and welcomed his embrace. It took some time, but her tears finally stopped.

"I'm so embarrassed I left your house that way. Please forgive me."

Eion took both her hands and gazed at her. "It's us who should plead for forgiveness. I see how much Caden loves you and I didn't want to give you another chance to leave town. I didn't mean to be meddlesome. Well, maybe I did, but it was in the name of love. You and Caden are perfect for each other. I see the looks you exchange, and the way my son's eyes sparkle when he sees you. I also know his heart ached when you disappeared. For the record, the women demanded to change and get ready, but I had a fear in my heart that outweighed my good sense. We all care for you. Please don't leave."

She peered into his eyes and saw his truth. She nodded. "Walk me back in?"

Epilogue

A *year later*

Laura Lee couldn't help the smile she'd worn all day. Caden was taking forever to reach home, and she had news. Earlier that morning, the doctor verified her suspicions. She couldn't be happier.

She heard a rider coming, and she rushed to the front door. It wasn't Caden, and she had to blink hard.

"Jaime, is that you?" She grinned in delight.

"Sure is. I'm in a bit of a pickle. I need to speak to you and Caden about."

A baby's cry came from the bundle he carried.

"What's that?" she inquired, stepping closer.

Jaime handed her the bundle before he got off the horse.

"She's the pickle." He took the bundle back and unwrapped the small infant girl.

"Is she yours?" Laura Lee caressed the side of the baby's face.

"No, but I was the only one alive who would take her. There was a bit of trouble at the ranch. Marshalls arrived, and Henry fought to the end."

"Come and sit down." Laura Lee moved up the few steps to the porch. She perched in one of the chairs. "Can I hold her?"

Jaime followed her and laughed. "Of course you can." He placed the baby in her arms and sat down. "It's Tierney and Henry's baby. Tierney gave birth during the shootout. All the women slipped out of the house. It's not like Tierney made any friends. They shot Henry early on, so I carried Tierney down to the root cellar. There's a cot down there for prisoners. Anyhow, this sweet girl was born."

"Where's Tierney?"

"I hid us from the Marshalls in the cellar and we remained until the next day to go aboveground. Tierney seemed to be a good mother. After three days, Tierney wanted to escape the mountain. I saddled her horse first, and she yelled, 'see you.' I searched but never encountered her."

"Oh, how could she?"

"It was Tierney being Tierney. I stopped at a few farms, and I was able to get her goat's milk. I didn't realize how many people have goats. Laura Lee, I can't take care of her. You were the first one I considered. I knew you'd get married to Caden."

"Jaime, I just don't know what to say."

Caden rode up and jumped down. He immediately moved to Jaime's horse and hugged it around its neck. "I never expected I'd meet you again. Rumble, where have you been?"

He walked onto the porch and shook Jaime's hand. He then kissed Laura Lee on the cheek.

"When did you get married, Jaime?" Caden asked.

"He's not. This is Tierney and Henry's child. Henry is dead and Tierney took off," Laura Lee explained.

Caden sat down. "I don't understand."

Jaime clarified the situation for Caden.

Caden stared dumbstruck. "What do you mean, you need to leave the baby here? My horse is staying."

"I'll hire a horse and ride to the orphanage. There's one in town. You two don't have children?"

"No, we don't." Caden narrowed his eyes. "Let me locate a horse for you." Caden left and continued to the barn.

"Your husband isn't as fond of me as I remember," Jaime chuckled.

"He's the jealous type." Laura Lee set the baby against her shoulder and rubbed her back. "What's her name?"

"Julia, after my mother. Tierney didn't bother to name her."

"I'm going to talk to that husband of mine."

The look of anger on Caden's face unsettled her. He glanced up and their gazes clashed.

"I have some news," she announced.

"Did you tell him you'd accept his baby?" Caden pressed.

"No, this is a surprise just for you and me." She sidled up to her husband. "I'm pregnant. The doc confirmed it this morning."

His face transformed into a look of awe. He folded her in his arms and lifted her off the ground. "You've made me one happy man."

"I couldn't wait for you to get home so I could tell you, but..."

"Maybe the two are connected. Maybe we're double blessed," Caden told her.

"Oh, thank you! Let's tell Jaime now!"

———

Later, after Jaime left with a different horse, Caden leaned against the barn door. His view was perfect. Laura Lee's happiness radiated from her as she sang to Julia. Having a baby in her arms suited her. Soon enough, they'd have another to hold.

He never expected discovering true love. He never thought he'd trust a woman enough. Laura Lee entered his life, turned it upside down, and then turned it right again. Not just right, better. God had been there every step of the way.

Caden had faith God would be with them for the rest of their lives.

Author Note

There were a number of "remedies" for snake bite in the 1800s, before the advent of antivenenes. How did they treat a rattlesnake bite in the 1800s? - Answers

- Frontiersmen believed that to put gun powder on the bite and set it alight would burn the venom right on out.
- Ammonia was a common remedy through the 1700s and 1800s. many people took to carrying a small bottle of ammonia when they ventured into rattlesnake country, which they could apply to the bite.
- A very painful but common remedy was to get a knife and cut out as much of the wound and (hopefully) the poison as possible.
- A poultice was sometimes applied, which could be made of a variety of materials, such as bark and gunpowder.
- There was even a belief that drinking a great quantity of whiskey would counteract the snake poison: what

they didn't realise was that alcohol only speeds up distribution and absorption of snake venom.

About the Author

Kathleen Ball is an USA Today Bestselling Author who pulls her readers into each story. She loves to write about flawed characters and how they change for the better. Her books have happy endings, it's the story of getting there that enchants her readers.

Visit my website Kathleenballromance.com

facebook.com/kathleenballwesternromance

twitter.com/kballauthor

instagram.com/author_kathleenball

tiktok.com/@kathleenballromance

amazon.com/author/kathleenball

Other Books by Kathleen

Faltered Beginnings

Fairer Than Any

Romance on the Oregon Trail Books 1-3

Cora's Courage

Luella's Longing

Dawn's Destiny

Romance on the Oregon Trail Books 4-5

Tara's Trial

Candle Glow and Mistletoe

The Kavanagh Brothers Books 1-3

Teagan: Cowboy Strong

Quinn: Cowboy Risk

Brogan: Cowboy Pride

The Kavanagh Brothers Books 4-6

Sullivan: Cowboy Protector

Donnell: Cowboy Scrutiny

Murphy: Cowboy Deceived

The Kavanagh Brothers Books 7-10

Fitzpatrick: Cowboy Reluctant

Angus: Cowboy Bewildered

Rafferty: Cowboy Trail Boss

Shea: Cowboy Chance

Mail Order Brides of Pine Crossing

Alanna

Briana

Aggie

The McKeegans

Aiden

Brayden

Myles

Caden

A Cowboy's Chance

Burke's Sweet Beloved

Clint's Sweet Calamity

Sweet Lasso Springs

Garrett